FURY

JORDAN MARIE

FURY

Savage Brothers MC—Tennessee Chapter

By

Jordan Marie

BLURB

Fury

I was sent to Florida on a mission. I'm here to help my club and my brother.

Devil has been through hell, he's found happiness with his old lady.

He has the life I've always wanted and tasted once...*briefly.*

I never dreamed trying to find someone for my club would lead me back to my past, and to the only woman I've ever loved.

Ellie Lane.

I claimed her as mine and gave her everything I had.
Losing her nearly destroyed me.
I don't know if I'm strong enough to let her go twice.

Ellie

Walking away from Liam was the hardest thing I've ever done.
Every day we make choices.
When it comes to Liam, I'm pretty sure I made the wrong one.
I never expected to see him again.
I still love him.
He still wants me.

I've dreamed of a second chance. It happens in fairy tales, right?

Although, I'm pretty sure the princess never got her prince under a hail of gunfire...

PROLOGUE

ELLIE

I thought I could handle it. I really thought I could. I'm not in the club life, or I wasn't before falling in love with Liam. Maybe I was young and stupid, didn't realize exactly what being in the club meant. I've put up with a lot, changed my whole world to fit in with Liam's and I didn't say a word. I didn't care. The club was part of him, so I could accept it. There were parts I even liked. But, I've finally had enough.

A woman can turn a blind eye to a lot of things, but hearing Diesel order a hit on another woman is hard to overlook. Admittedly, I don't like Vicki. I never did. But she's a human. She's a woman. She's not one of these guys that sells out a brother or fucks over the club for money. She wants custody of her son. That's it. Diesel ordered his men to find her. He wants her dead, either by his hand or his men. I can't ignore that. You fight for custody in court. You let the court know what a whacko your ex is. You don't order a hit on them. The fact that Liam so calmly accepts it scares the hell out of me.

"You can't do this, Liam."

"Stay out of it, Ellie. I love you, but I've told you before how things are. This concerns the club, not you. You aren't even supposed to know what's going on."

"The man I love is planning on killing an innocent human being. I think that involves me."

"There's nothing innocent about that tramp, Ellie."

"You can't do this, Liam. You just can't. No matter how bad she is, you can't kill Ryan's mother. Let the courts handle this."

"It's none of your business, Ellie."

"None of my business?" I snap. His words feel like a slap across the face, but more painful.

"Ellie, damn it, I don't want to discuss this with you," Liam growls. His words bounce off of me, because the pain is moving too deep for me to focus on what he's saying.

"Is this how you'll deal with me, Liam?"

"Woman, what are you talking about?" he yells. I can tell I'm making him mad. Liam is intimidating most of the time, although he's never tried to intimidate me before. He's always handled me with care, even when arguing. Now? Now he's just getting pissed. Probably because he feels trapped. Men hate that.

"What happens if we have a kid and break up, Liam? Will you—"

"Christ, woman. We're not breaking up," he rumbles under his breath, shaking his head at me.

"What if we did? What if you don't want me to have custody of our child? Will you calmly order your club to take me out, too?"

"You're not a crackhead whore, Ellie. Now, I'm tired of talking about this shit. I have a job to do and I'm going to do it. You need to step back from this and let it go. What happens is club business. It's not—"

"Yeah, I got that. It's not my concern. You said that. I only have one question, Liam. Will it concern me when the man I love is in jail for murder?"

"That won't happen, Ellie."

"And if it does?"

"Then, we'll deal with it," he says with a sigh.

"We'll deal with it..." I repeat, not able to believe what I'm hearing.

"I've got to go. I'll be back sometime next week."

"If you leave, I won't be here when you get back, Liam."

"Don't start that shit, Ellie. We'll work this out when I get back and you will be here," he orders, his voice gruff. It's full of anger and frustration, but even through it I can hear his worry. He loves me, I know he does, but he loves his club more and that's always been the case. I've been lying to myself, because now I know the truth.

I can't accept coming in second to his club.

Not anymore.

Liam steps into me, his hands going on either side of my face and he pulls my mouth roughly up to his, kissing me.

Liam's kisses always make my heart quicken. Even after all this time together, each kiss is like our first one. It never stops feeling new and exciting. I always feel my heart quicken and my skin tingle. My breath has to be pushed from my lungs, because it feels so good that I forget to breathe. From day one, Liam has been my everything. I thought I could accept being the second-most important thing to him.

Maybe I could have.

But, everything has changed now.

Everything.

When we break apart, his steel gray eyes bore into me.

"I love you, Ellie."

His words break my heart.

"I love you, too, Liam," I murmur, each word painful.

"We'll work this out," he says again. I don't say anything. There's nothing left to say.

Then, he walks away without a second look.

I stand there, rooted to the spot, as he leaves. I watch until he's completely out of sight, praying that it's not the last time I ever see Liam Maverick again.

FURY

I watch as the three bikers pull in beside me, dust kicking up all around us. I hate the fucking desert. I hate being here. I want to get back to Tennessee. I'm too old for these damn road trips.

I keep my gun hidden. I'm not getting bad vibes out of these guys. They're not wearing a patch. Just bikers in general, and from the looks of their boots, they are weekend riders.

"What's the problem, man?" one of them asks. He looks to be older than me, salt and pepper hair, goatee, earring, and a sleeve tattoo that is a mixture of skulls and butterflies of all things. You wouldn't think those would go together, but even I have to admit it's a sweet piece of ink. I wouldn't personally wear it, but to each their own. Fuck, if I tried that shit, Devil would hand me my ass daily over it.

"Bike started sputtering about a mile back. I was hoping to make it to the next gas station, but it didn't work out that way," I respond, nodding at the other two. They don't look that different from the first guy, a little more preppy, and I notice all three are wearing wedding rings. I pull my gaze from that. Too many memories want to spring forth at the reminder of that shit.

Ellie.

How long is that fucking woman going to haunt me?

I'm starting to think forever.

"You got tools?" one of the guys ask.

"Just the one I was born with," I respond with a smirk while they laugh.

"Dude, everyone knows to bring their tool kit with them on their bike," one of them criticizes. I manage to not roll my eyes at the biker-wanna-be—*barely.* I'm not about to tell them this is a bike I bought at a fucking pawn shop about fifty miles back, because I got tired of renting a cage and feeling closed in. It's a piece of shit, not worth what I paid for it, and about as far from my sexy metallic green Indian Springfield as you can get. Still, I got to feel the air, breathe it in and feel free for the first time in weeks, so it was worth it...until it died.

I am supposed to be in Florida. I never planned on carting my ass out to Arizona. I hate this fucking state. It's too damn hot for one, and it reminds me of meeting Ellie. Ever since crossing the state line, I swear to fuck I keep thinking I see her everywhere. It's never her, but for a minute, when I look at a woman with white-gold hair, the color of a palomino's mane, my chest goes tight.

I haven't seen Wolf at all, but when I got to Florida the trail to Torrent's sister led to Phoenix, Arizona of all places. I tried to bow out. Returning to Arizona was not what I wanted, even if Ellie had never lived close to Phoenix. Her family does live about five hours north, in Page, Arizona. I don't even know if she's still there, but I figure she is. That's where her family lives and where she was living when we met.

God, that feels like a lifetime ago...and I guess, maybe it was.

"Your bike paid for?" I ask the biker that hasn't spoken while forcing myself to think about anything other than Ellie.

"Mine? Uh...yeah. Why?" he says.

"What will you take for it?" I ask him, looking at the Honda and sizing it up.

"Uh well…"

"What year model is it?" I ask him, eyeing it. It's the lamest bike here—and that's including the one that died on me. I also figure I could get it the cheapest. Plus, this guy doesn't enjoy riding. If I had to guess, I'd say he's a banker or works some other desk job. His bike is old, beat up and the only three-wheeler in the bunch—conversion kit, at that.

"Eighty-eight," he says, still looking puzzled.

Jesus, it's even older than I thought—and not in the cool vintage way that I like my fucking bikes. "I'll give you five grand for it."

"For my bike?" He looks astonished and maybe he is. If I had to guess, I'd say he paid no more than two grand for this piece of shit.

"The offer ends in about three minutes," I warn him, getting tired of waiting.

"You've got five grand in your pocket?"

"Let me worry about how I'm going to pay you. You going to take my offer or not?"

"I…uh. Make it six," the guy says, looking so nervous I'm afraid he might get sick. I take a step back, just to protect my boots.

"Five and you can have the pink slip to this piece of shit. Take it or leave it."

"Take it," he says, not even blinking.

"I'll drive this into the next town, get your money out of the bank and you'll sign it over."

"Are you going to ride on the back? I've never had a passenger before," the man says instantly nervous. The other two have been quiet, but I know they're following the conversation.

"Fuck, no. You ride with one of your brothers. I'll drive myself."

"How do we know you won't try to lose us on the road?" the banker-guy asks.

"There's no way I could outrun you on this thing. Are we

doing this or not? I got shit I need to be doing," I growl, tired of fooling around. I'll take off walking to the next town. It might take me the rest of the evening, but right now I'd prefer that to listening to them talk.

"You can ride on the back of mine, Stu," the guy with the tattoos says. After looking at me nervously, *Stu* tosses me the keys. I catch them and climb on the albatross, I shouldn't be buying. From the looks of Stu, he probably has this damn thing serviced religiously. I figure it is dependable and that's all I need. I just have to find Torrent's sister and get my ass back to Tennessee where I belong.

The farther away I get from memories of Ellie and anywhere her or her family might still be...the better.

FURY

I stare at the whiskey on my table and then fill my glass up again. The bottle is still half full, but I've lost count of how many times I've refilled my glass. I don't think it's been enough, because defeat is still bitter on my tongue. Torrent's sister is nowhere in Phoenix. I tracked down the church, gave them the information I found in Florida, only to be told that Torrent's sister—whose name is actually Rayne Meyers—had taken a job with a sister church in Chicago. My first thought was how many fucking sister churches are there? I've been traveling all over the fucking world and it's getting old. My second thought is that I failed Devil and Torrent. I wanted her to have her sister safe and home before Christmas. Calling them tonight was the hardest thing I've done in a while. Devil told me not to worry, that he and Gunner would handle it, but I know the last thing he wants to do is to leave his woman right now.

At least I got answers. That wasn't easy—not by a longshot. There's one thing about these damn nuns. They protect their own. I can respect that. Luckily, when I showed them Torrent's letter her father left that explained about her sister and the danger she might be in, they let me know that Rayne wasn't there and where

I could find her. I also got their word they wouldn't share that information with anyone else and was reassured that no one had been there searching for Rayne. That at least made Torrent feel a little better. I've got to find Wolf, though. He's been in the wind for way too fucking long. The bastard needs to die.

I take another drink on that thought. I really thought I'd find him here in Phoenix. He had definitely been in Florida. Scorpion found that little nugget out when a woman came forth to the local police saying he had raped her. I met the woman, she'd definitely had the shit beat out of her. It is just another reason that Wolf needs to die. I tracked him down to a shack that the bastard had been staying in. It was empty, of course, and sitting next to a swamp. I'd hoped he'd been eaten by a gator, but sadly that wasn't the case. Scorpion was able to get security footage of the fucker buying a ticket at the airport in Jacksonville. We couldn't find out what name he was using or where he was going on our own, but with some help from a connection with the Florida State Police, it was clear he was headed out this way, though not Arizona. He bought a ticket to Texas. I should have flown there maybe, but when we got information on Rayne, I decided to get to her first. Now, I have nothing but a half-empty bottle of Jack. I'm feeling pretty fucking empty on my own.

Hell, I've been lonely since Ellie left. That woman owned a piece of me and I doubt that the void she left will ever be filled. I talk a good game in front of my brothers, but it's all bullshit. I'm grieving for a woman who walked away from me without a second look. Fuck, the last thing I need to think about is her while I'm drunk. It's probably just because I'm so close to where her family lives. I never tracked her down. She walked away and fuck it. If I didn't mean more to her than that, I didn't want her. I let her go. For all I know, she could be in Alaska, freezing her tits off. That'd be a shame, because they were fucking good tits. I used to love thrusting my cock between then and painting her face in my cum. Ellie was a gorgeous bitch with soft, gorgeous hair. But, she never bitched about me messing her hair up in bed. She didn't give a fuck if I bathed her in my cum. She loved sex. She loved anyway I gave it to her and most of the time it was as dirty as I could dream up.

Christ. I'm getting a fucking cock stand just remembering my time with her. All this time my dick has been mostly dead—despite what Devil and the others think. Now, that I'm rising to the occasion, so to speak, there's not a club whore around.

Just my luck.

I shove my chair out from the table, putting my hand down my pants, I wrap it around my cock and pull it up, because it's painful as fuck. The tip hangs out over my belt but that's better than where it was before. There's pre-cum on the head.

"Jesus, I need laid."

"I thought men were supposed to get limp when they drink as much as you are."

My gaze moves slowly over the woman with small, but firm, tits—nothing like my Ellie's. She's wearing a skin tight top and denim shorts. She's got thick blonde hair, not quite the same shade as Ellie's but it's long enough I could wrap my hand in it and feed her my cock. She's also got this deep shade of red lipstick on. My gaze stops there.

Plush, sugary-sweet lips, in a deep red.

The sight of them definitely reminds me of Ellie. *If I can't have her...*

One crystal clear thought begins to take root in my whiskey-fogged head.

"I'm not most men."

"Oh, I can definitely tell that," she grins. When she grins, her lips thin out and I frown in dislike. Ellie never had thin lips, fuck the more I kissed them they'd swell and somehow get even fucking sweeter. "Are you looking for some company?" she asks. I see it on her face. I'm fine with it. Hell, I can even respect it. She's not looking for a night of sex as much as the money it will put in her pocket.

"Not really," I tell her truthfully. Company is the last fucking thing I want. I don't want a woman in my bed at the hotel. I don't want to have to wake up and kick some bitch out in the cold. Still, I could use something to take the edge off tonight.

"Now, that's a damn shame."

"I like your lipstick," I tell her before she can turn away.

"You do?" she asks, with a startled laugh.

"Fuck, yeah. It makes me wonder."

"Wonder?" she asks.

"What it would look like on my cock," I tell her, taking another drink and judging her reaction.

Her eyes widen, but I don't think it's in shock.

"Well, I could show you…for a price."

And there it is. Cards on the table.

"How much we talking?" I ask her, putting my glass on the table.

"We can go back to your place and—"

"I don't have a place. I have a shitty-ass motel room that's barely fit to shit in. The last thing I want is a woman there. So, that's out."

"I could take you to my—"

"Here. I want you here."

"Maybe…the bathroom? Or at the back of the building?" she suggests

Now, I see the real shock on her face. I pull out my billfold, thankful I got some extra cash out at the bank. I didn't think this is what I'd use it for, but I'm damn glad. I take out a couple of hundreds and lay them on the table.

"Right here, right now. You, on your knees under the table, my cock stuck so far back in your mouth you're choking on it and you swallow down every bit of my cum and don't come up for air."

I see her body shiver. I don't know if it's for show. I also don't give a fuck.

She looks around the crowded club. I'm in the back, but it's not dark. There's every chance in the fucking world people will see her. I don't really give a fuck about that either. I take out another hundred, and put it with the others.

"Three hundred bucks to give you a hummer?" she asks.

"And swallow it down."

"You have a fucking disease I should know about?"

"Do you?" I return, not really caring. She doesn't look sick, not that you can tell from that shit. There's also a part of me that doesn't give a fuck what happens to me. I'm tired. I've been fucking tired for so long...

She reaches over and grabs the money, stuffing it into her bra. Her sadly slim tits show the money easily and I frown, visions of Ellie's full breasts that overfilled her bra every fucking time, float into my mind. Luckily, I won't have to see this girl's tits, because she'll be under the table.

"I'm going to rock your world. What's your name?" she asks.

"You can call me...Daddy," I respond with a grin. She laughs, then drops to her knees, crawling under the table. I reach for my glass, take another drink, then close my eyes as she undoes my pants.

Fuck, Ellie. This right here is all I need. Tomorrow, I'll meet up with Gunner and Devil in Chicago and I'll be doing it with a working dick. Maybe then, I'll finally be able to fuck her memory away.

ELLIE

"*E*llie, I've got bad news," Trina says, walking into the office. I hold my head down, not really wanting to hear it. I'm off work in…I look up at the clock on the wall across from my desk to confirm it.

Three minutes.

It's been a bad night, and the bar has been chaos, thanks to a bachelorette party gone wild in the party room. The last thing I want is more trouble. I want to go home, put on my jammies and crawl into bed, forgetting this entire day. What I don't want to do is deal with more drunk women or men who should have quit drinking an hour ago, but instead, are intent on ruining my night and drinking themselves into a stupor.

I might as well admit it. I hate my job. I hate it with a passion. Manager of Harvey Wallbanger's pays the bills. When I got the job, the name made me giggle. I met Harvey and even though he can be an asshole, I liked him. The job kind of sucks, but my schedule is decent and the money is good. Nights like tonight, though, make me want to throw in the towel and flip burgers at the diner down the street.

"Let Thomas handle it," I mutter.

"He's not here yet," Trina replies and I curse under my breath. That asshole knows it's time for me to be out of here. He also knows I can't leave until he gets here. *He just doesn't give a damn.*

"Is it really urgent, Trina? It's been a bad night," I mutter, rubbing my temple. I've got a migraine starting. They're nothing new, I get them often. This one, however, is going to be a killer. I can already tell.

"It's Hayley," she responds, disgust in her voice.

"Fuck," I hiss.

Hayley is a local girl, who gets her money by sleeping with the men who come in the bar. I'm not a prude and the way I figure it, prostitution has been around since the dawn of time. I can't judge it, because if a woman has to make money and this way offers her a better living, to each their own. My problem is that Hayley doesn't do it for the money as much as the thrill. She also doesn't care what or where she does it. Which means, if she gets Harvey's shut down because she's bare ass naked with her tits swaying in the air on the dance floor while she's taking it up the ass by some man with deep pockets, she couldn't care less—and trust me I know her tits sway because she's got five kids at home. If that wasn't proof enough, I've had to have the bouncers drag her and the Gibson brothers off the dance floor and out of the bar one night for trying to do that very thing. Personally, I would have banned all three from the bar at that point, but Harvey wouldn't let me. I suspect because Hayley let him do what I stopped the Gibson brothers from doing. Men are pigs. There's a huge part of me that doesn't want to go put a stop to Hayley's bullshit. It would serve Harvey right if he was reported and got shut down for a few days. The problem with that scenario is that most likely I'd lose my job, and since I'm partial to having a roof over my head, with food in my fridge…*it's not an option.*

"Jesus, doesn't that bitch ever take a night off?"

"Never. She enjoys what she does too much," Trina replies dryly.

"Women's bathroom again?"

"Nope, if it was there I'd have left you alone."

"Shit, the front door again?"

"Nope, and before you ask, not the bar top either."

"Now, I'm afraid to know. Harvey needs his ass kicked."

"Or his dick to fall off, which after messing with Hayley, it just might."

"Sorry, Trina. I know dealing with Hayley and her bullshit every night is the last thing you want to do," I respond with a sigh. Trina's ex, Tyler, is her ex because she came home from work one night and found him and Hayley in her bed.

"I wanted to take care of it myself, but I'd probably kill the bitch. Didn't figure Harvey would like a murder happening at his bar."

"Probably not. Where's she at?" I ask, picking up the phone and dialing without even thinking about the number—probably because I have to dial it too damn often.

"Table fifty-seven," Trina says.

"Thomas, where are you?" I ask into the phone.

"I'm about ten minutes out, Ellie. My car wouldn't start."

"I'd believe that if I didn't know you don't have a fucking car. I'm leaving in five minutes. You better have your ass here, or I'm telling Harvey that he needs to ditch your ass. I'm tired of covering for you."

"El—"

I hang up, and toss my cell on the desk, rubbing my temple. I definitely have a migraine now. I need to get home, medicate and sleep. I don't need to deal with this bullshit. I just don't have a choice. I stand up, grabbing my phone and shoving it into my back pants pocket.

"Time to take out the trash," I mumble to Trina.

"You can say that again," she says with a laugh, following me out.

ELLIE

"I don't see her."

"Under the table," Trina says. "Where you always find the trash."

My gaze goes down and sure enough, there is Hayley, under the table, her mouth buried between a pair of thick legs that are encased in worn jeans. At least this side of the bar is kind of dark. I can't see the man's face, but just from his outline I would say that Hayley's clientele has improved dramatically since the Gibson brothers.

I walk over and I'm almost directly at the table, when I hear the man groan out. "Quit teasing. Put it in that mouth of yours."

My knees threaten to buckle. I know that voice. I know it because it haunts me nightly. I stop, causing Trina to run into my back.

"El? You okay?"

I don't answer her. I'm not sure I could, even if I tried. It feels like I'm dying. I can't move, I can't look away. *I can't breathe.*

"El? Are you okay? You look like you've seen a ghost," Trina says. If I wasn't in shock, I'd hear the panic in her voice.

"Liam?"

I didn't mean to say his name. I sure as hell didn't want to. It slips out in my shock. I hope he doesn't hear me, but his face jerks around immediately and he stares at me, his silver-gray eyes cold as steel.

"Ice? What the fuck?"

I recoil when I hear his nickname. He used to think it was funny. He said my hair was so white it reminded him of ice, but I was so hot I felt like liquid fire when he was inside of me. I used to like that he thought of me like that and I couldn't deny it. My reaction to Liam was always combustible, it was so hot. Now? Now, I feel so cold that it hurts to drag air through my lungs.

But I do.

"Hayley, you've got one chance to get out from under this table and you two can continue your party in private, or I call Hank over here."

"Fuck, I'm just trying to make a living here," Hayley bitches from under the table, peeking her head out, spittle running along the side of her lips. I can't look at her. I can't look at that. I don't want to think of this whore with Liam's dick in her mouth. It shouldn't bother me. It's been over a year—hell, almost two—and it's not like Liam has even tried to get in touch with me—even after I served him with divorce papers. He calmly signed them and mailed them back to my mother's. I hated him for that and I know I didn't have a right to.

I still did.

"Trina, get Hank—"

"I'm getting out, you bitch. Maybe if you tried a fucking dick every once in a while, you wouldn't begrudge women who get them," she says crawling on her hands and knees. Considering that her shorts let her ass cheeks hang out, she's definitely giving Liam a view of what else could be his. To his credit, he doesn't look. He's too busy staring at me.

"Take your john and get out of my club."

"We'll see what Harvey has to say about this," the bitch huffs.

The urge to punch her is strong, but I resist. I don't want Liam to see that I'm upset.

"Well, he's not here. That means you have to deal with me. So you two get the fuck out of here and continue your party where my customers can't see you," I snap. I turn to walk away and Liam's hand wraps around my wrist, pulling me back around. I turn to look at him, the tension between us so thick that it nearly chokes me.

"What the fuck are you doing here?" Liam growls. My body jerks in reaction to the anger in his voice. My gaze rakes over him, taking in the subtle changes in him since we parted. Then, I drop my eyes down to take in his erect cock that is more than half out of his pants. Disgust, anger, and even jealousy wells up inside of me.

"Put your junk up, zip your pants and get the fuck out of my bar, Liam. If you don't, I'll have you arrested," I threaten. I turn away, closing my eyes briefly when he lets go of my hand. Then, I walk quickly back to my office. I don't stop, I don't answer Trina's questions. I just keep walking. When I get inside my office, I close the door, leaning against it, as my heart raps hard against my chest. I sink to the floor, as my legs finally buckle.

Liam is in Phoenix. Liam is in my bar.

Liam was getting a blowjob by a local hooker.

In *my* bar.

What does this mean? And why do I have the urge to run to my car and get the hell out of Arizona?

FURY

I let the nicotine fill my lungs. I let Hayley leave after she showed me Ellie's car. I've been standing here ever since. It's clear they hate each other, but considering she has three hundred bucks and doesn't have to do another damn thing for it, she left pretty happy. It figures it'd be my luck to finally get my fucking dick to work and run into the bitch who ruined me in the first place.

"When did you take up smoking?" Ellie asks, standing ten feet away from me. I reach up to take the cigarette from my lips, hiding the fact that my hand shakes when I see her.

I can't believe that after all this time, she's finally standing in front of me. I knew coming to Arizona was a bad idea. I should have called Gunner in sooner, hiked my ass back to Tennessee and continued forgetting this bitch...

I throw the cigarette down, grinding it out with my boot, my gaze never leaving her face. She hasn't changed. She looks exactly the same, which doesn't seem fair considering she nearly destroyed me and left me a fucking wreck.

"A man tends to pick up some bad habits when the woman he trusted with his life throws him over."

"Yeah, I saw your habit in the bar. I'd say stick to smoking. It's probably better for your health," she murmurs.

"Didn't know you cared," I say with a cold laugh that has nothing to do with humor.

"Do you mind stepping away from my car? I've had a long day and I just want to get home," she says, staring at me blankly.

No emotion, nothing. Just this matter of fact voice that is grating on my fucking nerves.

"What are you doing in Phoenix?"

"This is where I'm from, maybe you've forgotten, but I could ask you the same question. I don't need to though, do I? I'm guessing the answer to that would be the club. Did they send you down here to kill someone else, Liam? Damn, should I worry you've decided to off me because of the secrets I know?"

"Shut your fucking mouth, Ice."

"Yeah, I guess I should. Get the *fuck* away from my car and I'll do us both a favor and leave."

"You're not from Phoenix. How long have you been here?"

"Why do you care, Liam? In all that time you haven't bothered getting in contact with me once. I'm not about to play twenty questions with you now. Get the hell away from my car so I can make like a tree and leave."

"Christ. You're still corny as hell, Ice," I mutter, taking out another cigarette and lighting it—needing something to do with my hands.

"Liam, I have a migraine and it's going to be all I can do to get home. Your cigarette smoke isn't helping. Please, just step away so I can get out of here and put an end to this horrible night."

"You still get migraines? You really should see a doctor about those. They were getting more frequent before you left."

"They're brought on by stress. Funny how I develop one at the sight of you," she huffs and it makes me smile, although there's no joy in it.

"I figured you'd be living with your mom or sister. You always hated cities."

"Mom was driving me crazy and I'd rather have my fingernails pulled out one by one than live with Dawn and Glenna. Are you done with your twenty questions yet?"

"Glenna?"

"I guess that means we're not done with the questions," she mutters under her breath. "Glenna is Dawn's girlfriend."

Now that makes me laugh. Fuck, I laugh so hard that I almost choke as I toke on my cigarette.

"Dawn's a carpet muncher?"

"Liam—"

"I always knew that bitch hated dick."

"Well, she always hated you, at least. I can finally understand that. Are you going to leave, or do I need to get my bouncer out here to make you leave?" she asks, her features set and hard.

"You don't hate me, Ice. You might wish you did, but you don't," I respond, wanting to hear her admit it—maybe because I'm afraid I'm wrong.

"Leave me alone, Liam. You've managed to do that for way over a year now. For both our sakes, keep doing it."

I step away from her car. Her eyes dart to my face, but she quickly opens her door and gets inside. She slams it without saying goodbye. I didn't really expect it. Ellie is good at leaving me without a goodbye. I watch as she backs out and then heads out of the parking lot. She's right. I should let her go. Instead, I climb on my piece of shit bike and follow her.

Because I'm an idiot.

ELLIE

The club has barely opened and Liam was one of the first customers to walk in. He hasn't ordered anything, so I don't guess I can technically call him a customer. Instead, he walked in and stopped directly behind me. I'm standing at the bar, talking to my bartender, but I feel him there and I hate that my heart rate is intensifying and my palms are sweaty. I hate that being around Liam makes me feel alive again, because since leaving Tennessee, I've been existing just fine without the emotions he brings out in me.

"If you're looking for Hayley, she's been banned from the bar," I tell Liam when it's clear he's not going to move.

"Who?" he asks, sounding genuinely confused.

"The trick you paid to crawl under your table last night?" I remind him dryly, finally turning to look at him.

"I wasn't looking for her. I wanted to talk to you."

"Was it to tell me you were leaving town?"

"No."

"Then, I really don't want to hear it. I have work to do," I mumble, as I turn to go to my office.

"Don't you think we should talk, Ellie? It's been—"

"I know how long it's been, Liam. The time for us to talk was before the divorce was final. Now, it's over. It's the past and we leave it in the past." I hold my head down and pinch my nose when Liam follows me. I stop walking and turn to look at him. "I'm asking you to leave me alone."

"I just want to talk to you, Ice. Don't you think that after everything we should be able to spend ten minutes talking to one another without giving each other bullshit?"

I study his face, but as usual he gives nothing away. I finally let out a breath, giving in. It's clear that Liam isn't about to give up. There's one thing I know about him, he is like a dog with a bone. I might as well get this over with.

"Fine," I huff. "Ten minutes, but that's it and when we're done, you're leaving," I warn him. He doesn't reply, which should worry me. I lead him to the office and once he walks inside, I close the door.

"How did you end up managing a bar?" he asks, looking around my small office.

I let out an annoyed breath. "I don't want to do this with you, Liam."

"Do what?"

"Exchange small talk. How did you find me? Did you think it was funny hiring a hooker in my bar? Trying to get me back for leaving you? That seems petty as hell, especially after hearing nothing from you since I walked out."

"I can see your opinion of me hasn't improved in the time we've been apart, Ice."

"Is there a reason it should have?"

"You seriously asking me that shit, Ellie?" he asks, sliding his ass on my desk, ignoring my crap he's pushing back or the papers he's wrinkling. "Fuck woman, we lived together for two and a half years. Don't you think in all of that time you should have at least known me a little?"

"I know you, Liam."

"It sure as fuck doesn't sound like it. It sounds like you don't even like me," he mutters, his gray eyes cutting into me.

"Jesus Christ and cockleshells, Liam, what's the point of even getting into this now? It's over. Why are you even here? I don't see or hear from you for over a year. You send our separation agreement by certified mail and there's no note or anything. What does any of this even matter anymore?"

"I forgot the bullshit you used to say when you were upset," he murmurs, smiling at my make-believe curse word. I roll my eyes and say nothing. "I never did get a copy of our divorce decree," he says, his voice going quieter.

"You should have contacted the courthouse and requested a copy. It's not my place to take care of that crap for you anymore."

"I didn't really want to see it. Seeing it would have made it more real, Ice."

"We've been apart for almost two years. It can't get much realer than that, Liam," I respond, my words tight because there's a pain blooming in my chest I haven't felt in months. I really can't handle being this close to Liam again. I've always been too vulnerable when he's around.

"I never wanted this, Ice. I thought we were forever," he says. I close my eyes at the bittersweet quality to his voice.

"We're just too different," I tell him, my voice heartbreakingly sad, as I try to breathe through the heaviness in my chest.

"That's one of the things I always loved, Ice," he murmurs, stepping in so close to me that I can smell his aftershave. "Don't you remember?" His finger strokes against the side of my cheek. My eyelids get heavy, my body sways toward him, but then I jerk myself out of the haze he draws me into. I take a step away from him.

"I remember it's over. I remember you had another woman sucking your dick last night and probably have quite often since I've been gone. I remember we're divorced, but most of all I remember that we tried to make it work and it didn't."

"You expected me to swear off women after you left me, Ellie?" he laughs, but he doesn't sound humorous.

"Not at all. I actually figured you fucked one of the club whores the day you came back and found I was gone."

"Maybe it's good we did get divorced then, Ice, because it's clear you never knew me at all."

He gives me a long, hard look that I can't decipher and then walks out. I don't know how long I stand there looking at the door, all I know is I have to resist the urge to cry...

FURY

"*Y*ou heading back home?" Devil asks, while my hand tightens on the phone.

"Man," I start, rubbing the back of my neck, lying back onto the pillows in the cheap motel bed. I stare up at the ceiling which is supposed to be white, but is more smoke-stained yellow with dark spots showing water damage scattered about like confetti. The place also smells like a gym locker room. In other words, *a real dump.*

"What's going on with you, Fury?"

"I just have some personal shit I need to wade through. I don't want to let you down but, I can't head out to Chicago right now."

"Asshole," Devil growls. "Stop. You've put your life on hold for a while now trying to chase down this damn thing. You got real leads for us, plus we know that Torrent's sister should be settled in Chicago now. Gunner is already there and I'm leaving out tomorrow. Stop worrying about it. Why don't you tell me what's going on with you?"

"Torrent's going to let you go to Chicago alone?"

"Fuck, no. She's demanding to go with me."

"Oh, hell. You can't let her do that. What about LD?"

"Do you know you're the only asshole that calls my kid that? His name is Logan, asshole."

"He's going to be a hell raiser like his dad. So his name should be Little Devil. Torrent didn't want me calling her son Devil..." I shrug, even though he can't see the movement. "I compromised."

"Whatever. It will kill her to leave Cannon behind. So, we're still fighting about it."

"Cannon?"

"Little Devil is hung like his dad. Going to be a chip off the old block that one."

"Christ," I mutter.

"We're talking hung like a horse," Devil brags.

"Let it go, Devil," I mumble, trying not to laugh. I miss my old buddy. It's hard for me to believe that I've only seen him a couple of times in a year. I've made finding Wolf a priority. It had to be, and I'm the only original member in the club that doesn't have a family that needs them at home. Doesn't mean I don't miss them like crazy. The club hasn't felt like home for a while, however... not since Ellie left. "How are you going to get Torrent to stay home?"

"Tie her to the fucking bed tonight and wear her out."

"You think that will work?"

"I'll keep her tied up. She'll think that means she gets my dick through the night. Which, hey..." He breaks off laughing and I shake my head. "And when she wakes up, after being worn out and barely able to move, I'll be gone."

"Who's supposed to untie her the next day?"

"Red."

"Rory must really like you."

"Fuck you. Everyone likes me. Now, tell me why in the fuck you're avoiding my question."

"What question?" I grumble, still stalling.

"Fury, quit being a fucking tool."

"Ellie's here," I finally respond, the words feeling like dead weight.

"Motherfucker."

"Yeah."

"How's she look?"

"Like a fucking queen. Christ, Devil, I forgot just how fucking beautiful she is."

"She always was a looker. Still have that mouth?"

"Gives you hell just for breathing, yeah..."

"Always liked that about her."

"That's because you and I have a type. Torrent is a lot like Ellie."

"Probably, except my girl loves this club."

"Yeah, except for that."

"It probably helped that Torrent saw how bad a club could be and the fucking nightmares that we try to shut down here, Bro."

"Maybe."

"What are you going to do?"

"Fuck if I know, Devil. I just know I can't leave yet. I could lie and say it's because there's still a chance Wolf is here..."

"But, you'd stay either way."

"I'd stay either way," I agree, closing my eyes. The minute I do, it's Ellie's face that I see. Yeah, I can't leave. My brain is too fucked up. The problem is I'm not sure I'll be able to leave Ellie at all.

"Stay safe and check the fuck in," Devil growls.

"Will do. Good luck wearing your woman out." I try and joke.

"Fuck off. I don't need luck for that shit. You forget who you're talking to. I'm the fucking king of fucking."

"A legend in your own mind," I laugh. "Later, Devil."

"Later, Bro. Keep safe."

"You, too."

I hang up, instantly missing the asshole. I love all my brothers in the crew, but I'd be lying if I didn't say that the blood runs deeper with Devil. Our connection is stronger and maybe that's why I've dedicated this past year to trying to find Wolf and ending my brother's nightmare.

I can't go to Chicago. I have to stay here and figure out my own head. If I don't, I'll be too distracted and Wolf will put a bullet in me before I get a chance to end his miserable life. That won't help Devil. I've got to get my shit together. I've been ignoring it for way too long.

I've got to deal with how I feel about Ellie… and how *she* feels about me.

Fuck.

ELLIE

"*D*o you realize you've been here every night for over a week now?" I growl at Liam.

"You've noticed," he says with a smirk.

"Cut the hogwash, Liam. What are you up to?"

"I think the word is probably bullshit, Ice."

"What are you up to? Why are you hanging around here all at once?"

"I want to talk to you. Shit, Ellie. I just want to spend a little time with you. Is it so bad that I'd like to be your friend? You're important to me. We meant a lot to each other at one time. Hell, you still mean a lot to me."

"You get how that's kind of hard to believe from where I'm standing, Liam?"

I sigh as I look down at the man who has practically been staying at the bar this past week. He's also haunted my thoughts. I can't seem to get away from him. Trina said he even comes in on my nights off. When he finds out I'm not there, he leaves. It's confusing as hell. If he had given me all this attention when I first left, we might be together now.

Damn it! I'm a bitch for even thinking that. I left Liam. I made a choice. It's not one I wanted to make and during the time we've been apart, I'd be lying if I said I didn't regret it most of the time. I was scared. No woman wants the man she is in love with to be able to kill someone in cold blood. No woman wants to visit her man in jail for the rest of her life.

Unless the alternative means she won't see him at all.

How many times have I thought about that since I left? There were times that I ached for Liam. God, what is wrong with me? I was just starting to finally put him behind me and then...he showed up.

"You knew where I was all this time, Ice. You could have called or come back home. You had to know I would have welcomed you with open arms."

"Maybe at first. I'm not stupid, Liam and I had lived the club life for a while. I knew what would be available to warm your bed the minute I left."

"None of them were you."

"They were still pretty, warm, and willing," I tell him, the words hurting.

"When do you get off tonight?" he asks. His face is stern, his gray eyes almost piercing. I lick my lips nervously, raking my teeth against my bottom lip. I feel like I'm preparing myself to jump off a cliff. I know it's not a smart move, but it's something I want so much that I can't stop myself either.

"I'm off now. I'm getting a migraine, called the other manager in so I could go home. Plus, Harvey is here tonight. I'm not needed."

"Let me take you home."

"I've got my car," I tell him, this sinking feeling in the pit of my stomach that I'm making a mistake that I might not recover from.

"Then, let me follow you home. You used to say that I was the only one that knew how to help your headaches, remember?"

"We're not having sex, Liam." His full lips spread into a smile and his eyes seem to virtually heat. I ignore the way that makes me feel, or the fact I can feel my panties get wet. Liam's smile was always lethal to my well-being.

"I meant my massages, but Ice, I'd like nothing better than to sink my dick into you," he says, his voice dropping down into a throaty growl that sends goosebumps over my flesh.

Damn him.

"And that right there is why this is a bad idea," I tell him, shaking my head no. I start backing away from him, my fight or flight instincts finally kicking in. I'm running away and I'm not a bit ashamed to admit it.

"Let me follow you home and take care of you, Ice. I promise I'll be on my best behavior."

"Liam—"

"I mean it, Ellie. I'll be a freaking Boy Scout," he says, already getting up and letting me know that he's not prepared to take no for an answer. It's just my luck that I don't really want to say no...

"You do one thing I don't want, you're out of there and you don't argue," I mutter, knowing I'm doing the wrong thing, but unable to stop myself.

"You got it," he says, putting his hand at my back and leading me out of the bar. I glance up at his face, because even at five-seven, he towers over me. He looks entirely too satisfied with himself.

"You can wipe that smile off of your face. Even if I wanted sex from you—which I don't—"

"Liar."

"I'd never have sex with anyone who let Hayley near his dick. You'll be lucky if Fury, Jr. doesn't fall off."

"Christ, Ellie," he mutters, the look gone from his face. For a second, I resist laughing when his hand goes down to his crotch without thought. Maybe he's checking to make sure his dick is still attached. That thought makes it impossible to keep the laughter at bay. "You're such a bitch," he laughs. "Besides, you stopped her before she got to the good stuff, so *Fury, Jr.* is safe."

"You should thank me for that," I mutter, thankful we make it to my car so this conversation can stop. Suddenly, I don't want to think of Hayley under Liam's table. I don't want to think of Liam with any other woman because it hurts. I need to remember that it shouldn't. That we're not together and there's a reason for that.

I need to stop him from following me to the house.

But I don't...

FURY

"You're lying! Devil did not fall in love with a nun!" Ellie laughs.

God, I miss that laugh.

"He did. Well kind of, it's a long story. The point is that he's married and has a little boy now."

"I can hardly believe that. I would have thought Devil was an eternal bachelor," she says, shaking her head.

"He wouldn't be alive without Torrent," I tell her. I lose my train of thought as I stare at her.

I don't know how it's possible you can forget how truly beautiful a woman is, but my memory somehow pales in comparison to the real thing. Her white-gold hair is thick and long. It falls in soft waves around her face. One side of it is flipped over to the other, making my hands itch to run my fingers through it. Her plush lips give new meaning to the term bee stung, and her body still makes me hard with just a glance. That's not what draws my attention, however. It's her eyes, they're a blue, but a blue unlike any I've ever seen before. They're like the blue waters in Belize. I've never seen anything like them to describe it any other way. I had traveled to Belize once and the ocean there always stayed with me. From the moment I first saw Ellie, she brought those memories back. I even took her there on our honeymoon and made love to her on the beach as the waves crashed around us.

Fuck. I shift uncomfortably, resisting the urge to reach down into my jeans and adjust my cock. I don't want to piss her off. Ellie has a temper, she'd kick me out and that's the last thing I want. I need more time with her. God, I've missed her.

"Where did you go?" she asks softly. I yank my gaze back to hers, trying to focus.

"I'm sorry. Just thinking."

"About?"

"We went really wrong somehow, didn't we, Ice?"

"Yeah, we did."

"Do you ever regret the choices we made?"

"Sometimes," she admits. "I lied to myself, I guess."

"What do you mean?"

"I loved you so much, Liam. I thought I could overlook the life you led as long as it meant I could have you. But the deeper I got...the more it all felt out of control."

"You always did see things in black and white, Ice."

"Yeah, and you lived in those shades of gray."

"It sounds like a bad joke should be inserted here, but for the life of me I can't think of one," I joke. She laughs, though it doesn't quite reach her face.

"Just don't expect me to start calling you Christian."

"Thank God. He was a pussy."

"You watched that movie?"

"Against my will. Rory had the old ladies over to watch it while Diesel had to be out of town. He didn't like the idea of not having someone watch over his woman. I got the short end of the stick, since Devil was still in bad shape."

"Wait, hold up. Who is Rory and why was Devil in bad shape?"

"You've been gone a long time, baby."

"Yeah, I guess so. Life goes on, as they say," she lets out a big sigh that morphs into a yawn. I watch as she covers her mouth and smile.

"You're sleepy."

"I got up early. I hate to do this, but you should probably leave. I'm about to fall asleep on you."

"I could stay."

"Liam, I don't think that would be smart."

"I'll sleep on the couch," I suggest, but I can already see on her face that she's going to shoot me down.

"What if your headache comes back?"

"It's fine now," she replies, shaking her head.

"You had one the first day I saw you at the bar, Ellie. Are you seeing a doctor for them?"

"It's just tension. I have the day off tomorrow, I'll rest up and be right as rain."

I smile. "I've missed that," I tell her with an honesty I doubt she could understand.

"What?"

"The silly things you say. What does right as rain mean anyway?"

"Stop trying to confuse me," she says all while yawning, making it hard to understand her.

"Okay fine, I can take a hint, but I do have a favor to ask."

"What's that?" she asks, as I get up off the couch. She stands with me and I start walking—regretfully—to the front door.

"Go riding with me tomorrow."

"Liam..."

"C'mon, Ice. Live dangerously."

"I don't understand what your point is to all of this," she says so quietly that I have to strain to hear her.

"Why does it have to have a point? It feels good. You can't deny that, Ellie."

"So does drinking, but too much of it and you end up with a whore's mouth wrapped around your dick, a disease that you can't find a cure for, your nuts shriveled up, and a hell of a hangover."

"You're not going to let Hayley go are you?"

"If you want to escape my house with all of your body parts still in working order, you won't even mention her name in my house," she warns me, her eyes shooting fire at me.

"Jealous?"

"Don't come at me with that bullshit, Liam. I haven't liked Hayley for a long time. Did I like seeing her head buried between your legs? No way. Is that fair? Maybe not, but it doesn't change the truth. You don't love someone for years and have that just disappear, not if the feelings are real."

"Trust me, Ice. I know that," I tell her, my fingers drifting to the side of her face. I drag my finger along her soft skin. "Come out with me tomorrow. Please?"

"The mighty Liam Maverick actually says please?"

"Where you're concerned? Damn straight."

"If I go riding with you, it doesn't mean anything."

"Okay," I tell her, not adding that it does mean something. I'm about to get my way. Now's not the time to spook her.

"Okay? Just like that?"

"Just like that. Does this mean you're saying yes?"

"I'll probably regret it," she mutters. "But, yes."

I lean down and kiss her forehead. I breathe in her scent. It's sweet, even if I'd rather kiss her lips instead.

"See you tomorrow, Ice."

"Don't make me regret it," she warns. I don't turn around. If I did, she'd see me grin and that would just piss her off.

ELLIE

"*I* can't believe you're riding that thing."

I'm grinning as I say it, sliding off the back of his bike. Liam gets off with an ease that has been honed to a precision that is sexy and powerful. He always did move like poetry in motion. He takes my hand and I let him, without even thinking about it. It's a habit and one that you would think time would have broken, but yet it hasn't. At the very least, after all this time and the distance between us, I shouldn't feel my heartbeat quicken when he holds my hand. I shouldn't feel warm and happy just from his touch.

"Hey, don't knock this bike. It got me in town and to your bar," he mumbles.

"I think calling this thing a bike is an insult to all other bikes in the kingdom of Bike-dom, Liam."

"Bike-dom? I swear you really are a nerd, Ellie."

"You say that like it's a bad thing," I laugh, the exchange familiar, probably because we had it on our first date. That seems like such a long time ago.

"I think it's a really good thing, Ice," he murmurs, stopping and tugging on my hand so I'll stop and face him. His fingers sift through a strand of my hair that the wind has blown across my cheek.

"Liam…"

"I've missed having you in my life, Ellie. I've missed it every damn day."

"What are we doing?" I ask, feeling a little helpless.

"Whatever we want."

I look at him, trying to figure out why I feel like I'm drowning.

"None of this makes any sense. We're divorced. Your life is in Tennessee, Liam."

"Just because we're divorced, does that mean we can't be friends, Ice?"

"Is that what you want, Liam? To be my friend?"

"I sure as hell don't want us to be enemies, Ellie."

"I thought you would hate me for leaving," I tell him, quietly, whispering the words that keep me from sleeping at night.

"I think I did for a while," he responds with a brutal honesty that hurts, but then that's who Liam always was. He would tell you something flat out, it hurt at times, but you always knew where you stood with him.

"How long are you in town for?"

"I don't know. I just know I don't want to go back yet, Ice. I want to spend time with you and I think you feel the same."

"You do get that this doesn't make any sense, Liam?"

"We never did, but it sure was good, wasn't it, Ellie?"

My head drops down and I hide the small smile that pulls at my lips. This is crazy. *I'm crazy.* But, Liam isn't wrong. I do want to spend more time with him. Hell, I've wanted that since the day I left Tennessee. It hasn't changed, despite time. He's also not wrong. *It was good.*

"What now?" I ask him, getting up my nerve to return my gaze to his.

"I thought we'd play miniature golf. What do you think?"

I look over my shoulder at the place that Liam brought us to.

It's a miniature golf, arcade, and go-kart track. The kind of place we used to go to when we dated, and I grin. My man was always a giant kid.

My man.

He's not that anymore...*Is he?*

"I think I'm about to spank your butt," I respond with a grin.

"It's been a while, Ice, but don't forget, I'm the one that does the spanking in our relationship," he replies with a wink, taking my hand and leading me to the entrance. I ignore the quiver of anticipation that seems to center between my legs.

I'm playing with fire, but the heat of it keeps me from stopping. I have a bad feeling that it's too late anyway.

FURY

*S*he *still loves me.*
     I don't know a hell of a lot about love in general, but I know that. One week of spending time with her makes me pretty damn positive of how she feels. As for me? I've never stopped loving Ellie. I don't think it's possible. It doesn't solve the reasons we separated to begin with, but fuck…

I have to believe there's a way around it all.

I don't want to give my club up and I'm not sure I can give Ellie up. There has to be some way to meet in the middle.

It's been five days since we spent the day playing miniature golf and having fun at the arcade. Five days in which we've spent at least part of every one of them together. Tonight, I'm at Harvey's, waiting for her to get off work. She's filling in at the bar tonight, because her bartender called in sick. She's a natural behind the counter and I have to wonder why I never knew that. Ellie is just naturally good at anything she does. That makes it easy to overlook how good she is at anything she tries.

Fuck, I love her.

I took one look at her years ago and I've never been the same.

My gaze moves from her to the man she's talking to and

instantly I'm put on alert. I get up from my table and walk over to the bar without even thinking about it.

"Go out with me tomorrow night, El."

"Sorry, Wayne. I have to work."

"I can pick you up after work, I'm easy, baby."

Ellie laughs, puts a beer in front of the guy and gives him a smile that makes me want to punch something.

"I'm sure you are. But, the answer is still no."

I'm not a man used to feeling jealousy. Then again, I've never had to. Until Ellie, there wasn't a woman that I was possessive over. The minute I saw her, I claimed her. The attraction to her was so strong, I didn't bother fighting it. *I wanted her.* I wanted her in a way that I knew the feeling would last. It might sound stupid, but after just a week of dating, I had her in my bed and moved in with me. I told her that when a man saw what he wanted, he took it. She laughed at me, but she didn't argue either. In hindsight, maybe I should have slowed shit down. Maybe if she knew what kind of lifestyle I led, the things I did for the club in advance, she would have gotten time to sift through them and accepted that part of me. She could have kicked me to the curb, too, but it would have been better if it happened that way, instead of years down the road.

There's no going back, however. Ellie and I can only go forward and I want to do that with her by my side. My problem is convincing her to want the same thing. She immediately turns to another customer. I don't even know for sure if she saw me sit down. That's a damn blow to a man's ego. I used to be the only man Ellie noticed in a room full of others. I know it's been a while, but damn it, for her to act like she has this past week with me, she has to have the same feelings…

Fuck it, if she doesn't, she's going to have to learn to have them. I'm tired of pretending that I don't want my woman back.

I never hesitated before and she fell in love with me then. It's time I remind her of the man she married.

ELLIE

$\mathcal{I}$'m doing my best not to look at Liam. I know he heard Wayne ask me out. I can feel his heated gaze burning my back as I turn around to tend to another customer. I shouldn't feel guilty for a man asking me out. I shouldn't feel guilty for turning him down, but still being flirty. I shouldn't.

But, I do.

Which isn't fair and makes zero sense. Liam and I aren't married. It's been close to two years and I shouldn't feel like I'm cheating on my man, by enjoying it when a man flirt's with me. I mean, when I saw him for the first time in this bar, he was getting ready to get a blowjob from Hayley.

"Come on, Ellie. One date, what could it hurt?" Wayne asks. He's very persistent. He is most of the time when he asks me out. I've thought about going out with him once or twice. He's good looking in an all-American kind of way. He's funny and if what my waitresses say is to be believed, a good guy. I've always said no, mostly because I wasn't in the right headspace to be with a good guy. There's no point in hurting someone else, just because I'm messed up over my ex.

"Wayne, I have—"

i

"What she's trying to tell you, *Wayne*, is that she has a man and that man is *not* you."

My body goes stiff as Liam pushes his way into the conversation. My gaze travels up his body, to light on his face that's tight with an anger he's not bothering to hide. His gray eyes are molten steel and they're focused on Wayne.

"Is that true, Ellie?" Wayne asks, but he doesn't look at me. He's too busy watching Liam. From the looks of Liam's face, that's very smart.

"I—"

"Fuck, yes, it's true. Did I stutter, asshole?"

I haven't heard El tell me it's true and no offense, dude, I'm not going to believe shit until she tells me."

"You call me *dude* again, and you won't have to worry about what the fuck my wife says to you, you'll be too busy trying to pick your fucking teeth up off the floor."

"Your wife?"

"*Ex-wife*," I interject, recognizing that this whole thing is getting out of hand quickly.

"Wife," he growls.

"*Ex*," I growl back, just as stubbornly. Liam is still looking at Wayne, but when he hears me call him ex again, he turns to me.

"You're mine, Ellie. If this week has shown us anything it's that."

"I haven't been yours in almost two years, Liam. Did you really think a couple of dates could erase the Grand Canyon of problems we have?" I can't believe what he's saying to me right now. Here I was thinking that Liam had changed. Now I know he's still the same old asshole he's always been. It's always what he wants and how he wants it! "Thomas!" I snap.

"Yeah, El?"

"You're on duty," I tell him. "You, in my office now," I order Liam, so pissed that it's like a living burning thing inside of me.

"Sounds good to me. I like what happens when you get pissed, Ice."

That's not happening tonight," I huff. He can't seriously be insane enough to think that we are going to have sex in my office.

Liam crowds in behind me and out of the corner of my eye, I see him use his bicep to push Wayne out of my way.

"What the fuck, you prick," Wayne growls, standing up and preparing to take Liam on. "You want a piece of me, go ahead and try, asshole!"

"Go ahead, I'll give you the first hit," Liam responds, his voice sounding almost like he's on the verge of laughing.

Probably because he is.

"No one is hitting any one in my bar tonight. Wayne sit down. Thomas, give Wayne a drink on the house," I mutter, wondering how things went so bad, so quickly.

"You and me aren't finished asshole," Wayne yells and Liam flips him off. What he does next, however, has my mouth dropping to the floor and I literally have the urge to kill Liam.

"We can finish this after I fuck my wife and you sit there with your dick in your hand, *Wayne.* But hey, enjoy your free consolation drink," Liam says with a smirk. A smirk I want to wipe off his face.

So I do.

When he turns back around to face me, I'm staring straight at him. Maybe he can see that he's pushed me too far, but it's way too late.

"Ice—"

I straighten my hand out and slap him across the face so hard that my palm is heated from the impact.

"Fuck, woman."

"Not another word," I huff, so angry I'm shaking with it. I'm sick to my stomach because I struck Liam. I stomp off to my office. I don't know if Liam is following me and at this point, I'm kind of hoping he's not.

FURY

$\mathcal{I}$ follow her in the office, closing the door behind us and turning the lock. I stand against it, my face still heated from her slap. I cross my arms at my chest and look at Ellie. She's wearing faded jeans, a pale blue t-shirt that has Wallbanger's written across the front and her hair pulled back high on her head in a ponytail. Her hair is so long that the gathered strands still fall below her shoulders. The blue in her eyes are dark with anger. Her face tight, as she stares at me. Her breathing is ragged, causing her breasts to rise and fall and all I can think is that this is what I've been missing all this time. Ellie is electric. She gives life a purpose. Without her, I was barely existing. She brings heat, fire, and emotion. Fuck, I've missed her.

"You've got about three minutes to talk, Ice. After that, I bending you over that desk and spanking your ass for that little show out there."

"You touch me and I'll de-ball you in ten seconds. Don't forget that you taught me how to take care of myself, Liam and I'm damn good at it."

"I haven't forgotten, Ice. I also know that because I taught you, I know exactly what you will do. So, you're free to try. In fact, I want you to. The end result will still be the same. I'm spanking that ass of yours. You've got one minute."

I see the exact moment she begins to get uneasy. She's remembering who she's dealing with. I'm not like the boys she used to deal with, the ones that she could lead around with the crook of her finger. I'm a man and I never fit into any box she tried to put me in. That's part of the reason she fell in love with me. Hell, maybe it's why I fell in love with her too.

"You aren't touching me. We're *over* Liam. What you pulled out there was bullshit. If I want to go out with Wayne, or any freaking man, I will. There's not a thing you can do to stop me."

If you think that, you're in for the shock of your life, Ellie. You're mine. You've always been mine and I'm not going to pretend any longer that you're not."

"I'm yours?" she asks, disbelief making the words come out as a question, so I feel the need to confirm it and not leave room for argument.

"Mine."

"You're delusional."

I take a step towards her and she backs up, taking two away from me. Pretty soon she's going to crash into her desk, but since that's where I want her anyway, I'm more than good with that.

"Turn around and put your hands on the desk, Ice."

"Go to hell, Liam."

"That just bought you an extra slap."

"You take one more step towards me and I'll have Hank in here so quick your forking head will spin!"

"Forking?" I laugh, knowing that Ellie's strange words only make an appearance when she's nervous or pissed. In this case, it's probably both. It's kind of hard to tell which, actually. I like both looks on her, so either works for me. She flails around behind her, keeping me in her eyesight the entire time. She picks up the phone and holds it out like it's some kind of shield between us.

"You come one more step and I'm calling him," she warns.

"Who in the fuck is Hank?"

"Our bouncer." She huffs out the words like she's announcing that the current heavyweight champion of the world is going to come rushing in here to save her. What she apparently hasn't grasped is that no one can keep her from me. I'd take on the world to keep her. I've tasted time without her and I didn't realize how bitter it was, at least not fully, until I saw her again.

"He's welcome to try, but you and I both know he's not keeping me from you, Ice."

"Liam, be reasonable. We're divorced."

"You want another piece of paper between us, Ice?"

"Are you—"

"We'll go down to the fucking courthouse right now and get that shit done."

"You *are* delusional," she mumbles.

"I'm telling you that I don't care if it's been a year or—"

"Liam, it's been almost *two* years!"

"Or fifteen years, Ellie," I snap. "You're still mine. You've always been mine and you always will be."

"That's not how it works," she argues. "You can't say that and you *especially* can't say that shit now. The time to try and keep me with you was when I told you I was going to leave if you went through with Diesel's orders!"

"And I told you, we'd deal with shit when I got back. You packed up and left. You made your choice and what has become clear as fucking crystal to me is that it was the wrong one!"

"I...I don't even know what to say to you right now, Liam."

"Good, because the time for talking is done. Now, you bend over that fucking desk and you offer me your ass."

"Offer you my...Liam Maverick, if you come near my ass I'll gut you!"

"There's my Ice, so full of fire it could heat the fucking world."

"I'm not your Ice! I'm not anything to you!"

"You know better. There's no way in hell you believe that, Ellie."

"I do! You let me walk away, Liam. You didn't try to find me, you didn't call, nothing."

"Ellie—"

"You dismissed my concerns. You treated me like some weak-brained woman who would wait at home and do as you said. You didn't care that I was scared, and you sure as hell didn't care if what you were doing would destroy our relationship!"

"Is that what you're pissed off about the most, Ellie? Because I didn't come after your ass?"

"No!

"Liar," I growl. I have just enough time to duck before she throws the phone at me.

Yeah, my Ellie is definitely back.

ELLIE

I hate him. I hate him for so many things, but most of all right now, I'm afraid he's right. I mean, it tore my heart out to make the decisions that I had to make—that I felt forced to make. I grieved him and he didn't call to check on me once. *He didn't try to find me.* He's right, that's what cuts the most. I was so insignificant that he didn't try to even call me and yell because I left.

I've been stupid. This past week I've let him back in, all the while hoping something magical would happen and erase the past two years. It's not. Nothing is going to change what happened, nothing is going to change Liam.

Or me, apparently.

I'm still the girl in love with a man who takes the law into his own hands. I'm still the girl afraid of what his decisions could mean for our future. Except leaving him just assured that we have no future at all. The worst part is, I'm still here in love with him, but now I'm alone and miserable all the time.

And I am miserable.

I live on coffee and doughnuts. I rarely have a regular meal. I work constantly and it's not because I'm in desperate need for money, although that part is nice. It's because staying home alone gives me too much time to think and too much time to regret. I do regret leaving Liam. I had my reasons at the time, but my life now is not the same and I miss my husband.

"Stop overthinking, Ice and just admit it," he murmurs softly, his voice going a little tender. I close my eyes, feeling defeated.

"You didn't even call me, Liam. Not once. You let me walk away."

"I gave you what you wanted, Ellie. At least that's what I thought I was doing."

"Then, you need to do it again. There's too much time between us now and way too much butter in the gravy pan."

"I have no idea what that means, de-Ellie it for me."

I roll my eyes, but I fall short of smiling. There's definitely nothing here to smile about.

"Homemade brown gravy is better with bacon grease, but you have these people that make it with butter. It's a fine line, too much butter and it loses its taste forever. That's us."

"You're comparing us to a food that is made to clog your arteries and kills you?"

"Breakfast isn't breakfast without gravy," I remind him, "But, maybe that's a good analogy. We were something that tastes great on the tongue, but is overall bad for us."

"I don't know much about the horseshit you keep digging in, Ice. But, I do remember how great you did taste on my tongue. Starting every morning with my head buried between your legs was my life's goal. Fuck, if I don't miss that."

"That's just sex, Liam," I mumble, ignoring the way his words makes these nervous flutters in my stomach. "I'm sure you had me replaced almost as soon as I walked out the door. God knows, the club girls were all itching to fall on your dick while I was there."

"I warned you before, not to get that shit twisted in your head, Ellie. You're the only woman I wanted."

"You proved that while we were together. I'm saying once I left and wasn't an issue for you anymore," I defend, wanting him to know that I never worried about him cheating on me while we were together. He gave me his word and I always believed him. *Always.* Fury never lied to me. He always laid it out plain and simple. He just never bothered taking me or us into consideration when it mattered most.

"Is that what you did, Ellie? Did you replace me quickly? Did you let someone else between those sexy, long as fuck legs of yours?"

"We've been apart for almost two years, Liam. Did you think I'd never find someone to give me what you used to?" I taunt, feeling the anger inside of me begin to fester again. I probably chose the wrong words, though. Because I see his face fill with anger, his entire body tense, his muscles stretch against his tight skin. There's a reason the men nicknamed Liam, Fury. He's intimidating as hell when you push him to the edge and his anger takes over. I've never been afraid of him, but when he's like this, it's only smart to get cautious.

I move away from him, the backs of my legs hitting my desk, as I watch him closely. I've always said that Liam had a grizzly bear inside of him. It would seem that I've just poked the bear out of hibernation.

"Who was it, Ellie? Was it that fucker outside? Did you let him crawl between your—"

"Stop it, Liam. You don't have a right to ask me any of this," I snap. I've never been one to back down from Liam's rage and that hasn't changed.

"The fuck I don't." His voice is quiet but deadly. He walks until he's pressed against me, his hand at my neck. His thumb pushing against my pulse. "I don't care how long it has been Ellie, I was your first and you will always belong to me."

"That's bullshit and we both know it. Do you expect me to believe you haven't had one woman since we've been apart? What was that whore between your legs the other night? A figment of my imagination?"

"My dick hasn't been inside another woman since you left, Ice."

"You never lied to me when we were together, Liam. Don't start now," I snarl, his words are painful, because one of the biggest hurts I've had to deal with was knowing that by leaving, Liam would be free to give another woman everything that was once mine.

"You know me better than that, Ellie. The one time I decided to say fuck it and try, you show up. If that's not a sign from above, I don't know what the hell is.

"You want me to believe you haven't been with a woman since me?" I ask, torn between wanting to believe it and afraid of believing it at the same time.

"I'm not saying I didn't try at first. I'm saying when you left, my shit was left broken," he says, his lips stretching into an almost smile, that looks a little bitter.

"It didn't look broken the other night."

"And maybe it wouldn't have been if I'd let her finish. I can't say either way, what I do know is that once you showed up everything changed for me. These past few days have been so fucking good, I know I'm not giving you up."

"Liam—"

"And I know you need to quit trying to run away, Ellie. Running didn't work out before. Now we're here."

"I live here now."

"You liked Tennessee."

"My job is here."

"There's a job in Tennessee with your name on it, Ellie."

"I'm afraid to ask," I mumble, some of the tension I was feeling finally starting to bleed away.

"The pay sucks, but the fringe benefits can't be matched," he jokes, leaving no room to mistake what type of job he'd be offering.

"I can't promise anything, Liam, and honestly there's a real chance you might not want me now. I'm not the same person I was when I left."

"We can take it day by day. I'm not rushing you, Ice. But that fucker out there doesn't get one more taste of you."

"He never had one to begin with, you idiot," I mumble, still confused, but tired of fighting.

"Then—"

"I may have left you, Liam, but I still loved you. You know I'm not the type of woman to do the mattress mambo with someone unless I love them."

"You did with me after just three days, Ice," he reminds me. I can feel my face heat as I blush.

"I loved you," I sigh. "I've always loved you, Liam."

"So, once you left, you were broken, too?" he murmurs, leaning in to nuzzle my neck. I close my eyes, realizing he wants me to give him the words. I should resent that, but for some reason, I don't.

"Yeah, dummy. I was broken, too."

"That makes me unbelievably fucking happy, Ice."

"Because you're an asshole," I mutter.

"Probably, but I don't really give a fuck. But, I'm feeling the need to celebrate…"

"I have to tell you, Liam. I'm not ready to bend over my desk, so if that's what you're thinking, you can get that thought out of your mind for now."

"I can wait as long as you can," he says with a smirk that tells me I just might be in trouble…

FURY

"*D*amn it!" I growl, tossing my phone onto the table.

"What's wrong?" Ellie asks coming in from the kitchen.

"The guy I told you that I've spent the last year tracking?"

"Yeah?"

"Sister Evangaline just called. I showed her a picture of this fucker and told her he was dangerous. I told her to contact me if she heard from him."

"He showed up," Ellie murmurs.

"Yeah, Ice. I'm fucking sorry, but I'm going to have to cancel on dinner tonight and go over and see what is going on."

"Can't you go tomorrow?" she asks, watching me closely. If she only knew how much I want to tell her yes. I can't though. If there's even the smallest chance that I might be able to catch Wolf and end his sorry life, then I need to act immediately.

"He just left from there, Ice. If there's a chance that I can get this asshole, I need to."

"You're playing hitman again, aren't you?"

"Damn straight. This motherfucker deserves to die, Ice. He

almost killed Devil, he destroyed Torrent's life. I want him dead and I want him to fucking suffer when he does it."

"So the conversation we had yesterday, was just that, right? Nothing has really changed."

"I am who I am, Ellie. You know that. The club is part of me."

"And I just have to adapt and pray that whatever you do, doesn't destroy what we build together," she responds, watching me closely. I know this is a pivotal moment and a lot rides on it. I can't lie to her, though. If we go forward it has to be with her eyes wide open. So, I do the only thing I can.

"You leaving nearly destroyed both of us, Ellie. It didn't change how I feel about you though and I think you still feel the same about me. So tell me, is your solution any better than mine?"

"You don't have a solution. You just want to me to accept it and ignore the consequences."

"I want you to love me, Ellie. That's what I've always wanted. I want you to love me the exact same way I love you."

"Liam..."

"What are your biggest fears about me, Ellie?"

"That you'll always put your club first when it comes to us and do whatever they ask, not caring what it will do to us."

"That's a mouthful..." I respond, rubbing the back of my neck, thinking about what she just said. I let out a sigh as I devise a way to attack her fears.

"You asked," she says with a shrug, her gaze never wavering.

"Fair enough. How about you answer two questions for me, Ellie."

"I will try," she promises.

"What is it you're so scared of happening to me?"

"You mean besides you going to jail and leaving us separated for the rest of our lives?"

"Aren't we separated now, Ellie? You're making your worst-case scenario come true and I don't have a thing to do with that."

I watch as she considers what I'm saying. Her face changes and

I hope that means I'm getting through to her, but I don't have any way of truly knowing. I watch the way her throat works as she swallows, my gaze drawn to the nervous way she licks her lips. God, she's fucking gorgeous. Everything about her turns me on.

"Give me five minutes to change," she mutters, turning away.

"To change?"

"If you're going to this church searching for Voldemort, I'm going with you."

"Voldemort?" I ask, not knowing what in the fuck she's talking about.

"Harry Potter? The bad guy to end all bad guys?"

"No idea what you're talking about, Ice."

"Have you been living under a rock for the past ten years or more?" she asks, her mouth dropping open in disbelief.

"You're cute as fuck right now, Baby, but I don't want you near this fucker. He'd kill you without a thought."

"Then, I guess you're going to have to protect me."

"Ellie…"

"You want me to accept you're this biker who lives by his own set of rules? Then, you're going to have to let me try, Liam."

I frown, trying to intimidate her, but it doesn't work. She crosses her arms at her waist and waits.

"You always were shit when it came to minding me," I mumble.

"Oh, please, we were married, you weren't my daddy."

"It was fun when we pretended I was," I tell her with a grin.

"Down boy. We're going slow, remember?"

"We fucked for the first time on our third date. I've been here a week and haven't even got a kiss, Ice. If we go much slower my poor dick will shrivel up like a prune and be covered in dust bunnies."

"Oh, gross."

"That's what I'm saying."

"You keeping putting images like that in my mind and we'll never have sex again, Liam."

"Get that cute ass of yours upstairs and change before I spank it," I growl, my cock growing hard at just hearing her say the word sex. Hell, if I ever do get between her legs again, I may never come up for air.

"You're letting me go? Does this mean I've won an argument with you?" she asks, in complete shock.

"I'm showing you that I'm willing to change, too, if it means you come home where you belong, Ice. Now go, before I regret giving in."

"I love you, Liam," she says excitedly, shocking the hell out of me. Then, she kisses me quickly on the lips and bounces upstairs.

"Hey, Ellie?" I call out and she stops midway on the stairs and looks back at me.

"Yeah?"

"If you did something and ever ended up in jail? I'd still be the first to come and see you every fucking day they let me and I'd sign up for those fucking conjugal visits immediately."

"Liam—"

"If you think jail, or any fucking body, could keep me away from you, Ellie, you're wrong. The only person that has ever had the power to keep me from you...*is you.*"

She understands me. I can tell by the way my declaration makes her flinch. Slowly, she nods her head yes.

"I'll...just go upstairs and change," she says finally.

"You do that, Ice. You do that." I tell her. All I can do is hope like hell that I'm right that Ellie and I have turned some kind of damn corner tonight, because I'm afraid I'm lying. I told her the club was part of me and I'd never be able to give it up. But, after tasting life without her, I know as much as I'd hate it, I'd give everything up before I can let her walk away again.

I'm just not strong enough to let her go again. Maybe I never was. That's probably the real reason I never tracked her down. It's too late now. She's here with me and she's never getting away again.

ELLIE

"*The only person that has ever had the power to keep me from you...is you.*"

I keep replaying those words in my head over and over. Liam's not a hundred percent right, but what he says makes a lot of sense. I'm weakening, I know I am, but between everything he's saying and being on his bike, pressed up against him, my head lying against his back, as we move through the city, my brain is mush. I know how much I've missed Liam. I've ached for him every day, but I don't think I remembered how good things were between us during the happy times. Suddenly it's all coming back to me and this time around, I don't have this huge fear inside of me like I did before.

Of course, Liam doesn't know everything and when he does, he may hate me. But, he loves me right now. Plus, there's no reason he *has* to know. We can start fresh, erase our history and begin again. Isn't that what true second chances are all about?

We pull into a large, historical looking Catholic church with these gigantic towers that remind me of something out of a fairytale. Once Liam shuts the bike off, I slide from my seat, waiting for him. He immediately grabs my hand in his and I look down as our fingers intertwine. When my gaze moves back to Liam, he's staring at me, his eyes intent. He's studying me, I know enough about my man to know that he never misses a beat. I give him a smile, not a happy one, but a reassuring one. When he still doesn't make a move, I lean up to press my lips against his. I don't know why, I'm acting on instinct. It seems to be the right move though because he pulls me against him with his free hand, his other still joined with mine. He nuzzles my neck, kissing it. Then, his nose brushes against my ear and I feel his hot breath feather against my skin as he whispers, "Missed the fuck out of you, Ice."

It feels as if my heart squeezes tightly in my chest.

"I missed you, too, Liam..." I respond, my voice so breathy that I'm not sure it sounds anything like me. His words feel huge, as if they truly feed a soul that has been starving and that's exactly what I've been.

Starving for him.

It's not sexual, although that's always come naturally with us. It's so much more than that. He gives me joy.

We pull apart and walk up the steps to the church.

"Want to get married while we're here?" he asks. My heart beats hard against my chest. My first instinct is to say yes, and that should scare me.

"Very funny, Liam."

"Wasn't joking, Ice," he says with a wink. I don't respond, probably because I'm afraid of what my answer could mean. I'm not sure I'm ready to take that next step just yet. When we get to the front door he stops abruptly, looking down at me. His hand wraps against the side of my neck. "I'm supposed to have my mind on nothing but business right now, Ellie, but I swear to fuck all I can do is look at the way you've braided your hair to ride and remember the hundreds of times I undid it so it would fall around your face as I fucked you."

ii

"I'm not sure you're supposed to have this kind of conversation outside of a church, Liam."

"The way I look at it, Ellie, you're my gift from a higher power. What better place to give thanks for you?"

"I think I'd forgotten what a sweet talker you are," I mumble, feeling warm all over.

"I'm going to kiss you, Ice. It's not going to be sweet. I'm going to fuck your mouth with my tongue and all you're going to do is hold on for the ride, got it?"

"I...uh..."

"You don't have a choice, I'm just giving you a warning."

"Okay "

His mouth slams against mine before I get a chance to say anything else. His tongue thrusts inside, wrapping around mine. My legs get immediately weak. Instantly the taste of Liam brings back memories that I could have sworn I'd never forgotten, yet somehow they feel brand new. I collapse against him, giving my weight, as he plunders my mouth, taking it over and owning it. *Just as he owns me.*

When we break apart, both of us are breathing hard. My heart is hammering so hard in my chest that it should be painful. I slowly open my eyes to look at Liam. He's right in front of me. *Present. Intense. Mine for the taking.*

"Let's get this done," he says, his voice so deep and dark that I shiver.

"Uh..." I stumble to find more words, afraid I've done something wrong.

"Ice, we need to hurry or I swear to God, I'm going to fuck you right here on the steps. I'm pretty sure that's something you don't want to happen."

"We're next to a park full of children, so maybe not."

"They'll need a lesson in the birds and the bees sooner or later."

"I vote later," I mumble.

"Figured. Let's get this shit done, then."

"Okay," I agree. I try to give him a smile, even though my brain is frazzled.

He gives me a quick kiss, sadly no tongue this time. "Okay," he says, leading me inside.

WOLF

That fucking nun was lying. I knew the moment she shot me down, that she was expecting me. I'm getting so tired of this shit. I spent a year with my head down, because I know that fucker Devil has a price on my head. I'm too smart for them, I always have been. That's why I'm still alive.

I escaped the day Diesel got his revenge on King, then made my way to Florida. I didn't really have direction. I was definitely at loose ends. Figuring out why Diesel had a man in St. Augustine seemed like as good a reason as any to head that way. I was hoping to find a way to make Devil and Torrent even more miserable. I never dreamed what I'd really stumble upon.

Layla had another daughter. Dodger never breathed a word of it, but I stole the fucking papers at the orphanage myself. Rayne Meyers was the girl's name and Dodger signed her in as her father. That fucking whore told me she wasn't sleeping with Dodger any longer. I should have known she was lying. Of course she could have been lying to Dodger, too.

There's a very real possibility the girl is mine. It's become a goal to find her now. I don't know what I'll do with her. Maybe she is mine. I don't want her. She has Layla's blood and in the end she'll be just as weak as Torrent is. Maybe I'll keep her and send Devil and Torrent pictures of me torturing her. Torrent won't be able to handle the guilt. It's just a bonus that she'll realize that sorry sack of shit she's tied herself to is too much of a cripple to protect her family.

That could definitely be fun.

I'm close to getting my hands on this Rayne, too. I followed Charles Liam Maverick, or Fury, as he's known in Devil's club, to Arizona. Having gotten the information the nun gave him, I knew where he was headed, but I still found a certain amount of pleasure in the fact that I always stayed close to him. Fuck, I even ate in the same restaurant with him once or twice. The fucker had no idea.

The nun hadn't wanted to tell me the information she gave Fury, of course. I have to say, for a nun, the bitch put up a pretty good fight, but I found the right buttons to push. I even killed her and put her out of her misery for finally cooperating. The bitch should have thanked me for that, there were other things I thought about doing to her.

I should have come to the church in Phoenix before Fury. That was the plan, but I discovered this sexy blonde with thick lips, big tits and an ass that begged to be fucked. I thought I had time after rigging that fucker's bike. I thought at best, he'd die in the desert with the vultures circling him. At worst, he'd be stranded for a few hours. I was obviously wrong. I swear that asshole is luckier than Devil was. I eventually caught Devil, though, and he didn't feel lucky at all by the time I had my fun. *Neither will Fury*. I just needed to find his weakness. All men have them, even me. I didn't think I'd find Fury's so easily, but from the kiss he just laid on the blonde with him, I say I've found it.

This is going to fun...I always did like blondes.

FURY

"I don't think Diesel took that well..."

I look up at Ellie, almost guiltily, because I forgot she was there. I've been alone on the road for so long that discussing all this bullshit with Diesel somehow made me feel isolated all over again.

"That's an understatement, Ice."

"He should tell Devil," she says frowning, her blue eyes reflective as she thinks through the conversation I just had. It's strange, but I know immediately that's what she's doing. Then again, Ellie always took her time, weighed every alternative. Maybe that's why she never wavered from her opinion or decisions. It's one thing I've always loved and hated about her. Loved, because it showed what a beautiful, smart woman she was. But, I hated it because I knew that she went through the exact same process when she left me. That meant she knew the consequences and pain, but was still set on leaving me. That shit fucking crushes a man.

"Maybe," I admit, still not comfortable with keeping it from Devil.

"No maybe about it. Wolf almost killed him, he tortured his wife and came close to destroying his life. It should be him dealing with Wolf, not you."

"If this is some kind of bullshit to get me not to kill this motherfucker, Ellie, you can forget it. I get the chance and Wolf is gone."

"Do you see this look on my face, Liam?"

"The pissed off one that makes me wonder if I should hide my fucking balls?"

"That's the one," she says, way too sweetly. "You make it sound like I'm totally against your way of life and the club in general. It was never that."

"You're against the things I do for the club, Ice. You can't deny that."

She lets out a big sigh and flops down into my lap. She curls so her head rests against my chest. I hold her close, tucking her head under my chin and breathing in her scent. I'm frustrated as hell. I hate that Wolf might be anywhere near Ellie. I should have never let her go to the church with me. But, right now she's in my arms and I've ached for her for so long that I just try to concentrate on that and let some of the tension out of my body.

"Your life scares me, Liam. I can't deny that. I also know that there are things that need to be handled, because your world is different. You've told me about what happened with Devil and I may not like it, but I can see the necessity of it. Because if Wolf is still searching for Torrent's sister a year later, he's not going to just let it go. Plus, there's no way to prove he's done anything illegal. It will be his word against Devil's, or other members of the club. I'm not so stupid that I don't remember how the law treated the club in general. So, I get it."

"Why do I hear a but in there, Ice?"

"Because you're smart?" she jokes, kissing my neck.

"Let me have it, Ellie."

"If you guys keep this from Devil, after the hell that Wolf put him through, he won't forgive you."

"He's still having health issues for all of the shit he went through, Ice. Damn it all to hell, he has a new son and a wife he adores. He needs to enjoy life, not let the past rear up to fuck with his head again."

"So, what's the plan? Kill him and give his corpse to Devil as a christening present for Logan, Jr.?"

"Devil would appreciate the gift," I defend, grinning because it feels good talking with Ellie again about life. Hell, it feels good just having her in my arms again.

"No, he wouldn't. What if the roles were reversed, Liam? Would you appreciate it, or would you feel cheated?"

"Ice," I growl under my breath. There goes that mind of hers again. Sharp as a fucking tack. She's absolutely right.

"Hah! There it is!" she cries, pulling away from me to look at my face.

"What are you talking about, now?" I mutter, loving that her lips have spread into a smile that reaches her eyes.

"That tone you get when I'm right, but you don't want to admit it."

"And there's my old lady, the ball buster," I grumble, good-naturedly.

"So, this woman said that Wolf came asking about this girl Rayne. How do you know he won't just give up? There's a chance he doesn't know this is his daughter, right?"

"Maybe, but if he knows enough to ask for her by name, then chances are he knows it's his daughter. At the very least, he knows that she is Torrent's sister and he can use her."

"You don't think he'll give up and just drop out of sight?"

"No. Men like Wolf are only happy when they have power. He wants the power to torture Torrent again. He won't give up."

"Torrent? You don't think it's Devil he wants to torture?"

"No. He hates Devil, but for him the best part of hurting Devil was what it would do to Torrent. He wants his power over her. Maybe he's transferred his obsession with her mother to Torrent, I don't know. I don't want to find out."

"Is there a chance he'll transfer it to Rayne, Torrent's sister?"

"You're asking me to figure out a crazy man's thought process, Ice. Who knows? But, I do think there's a good chance."

"What happens next?"

"I spend my days camped out at the church, watching for Wolf to show up again."

"That's the big plan?"

"You got a better one?"

"Not really, but that sounds boring as watching mud dry."

"Have you watched mud dry?"

"Nope, it'd be boring, that's my point."

"You're goofy as hell, Ellie, but damn if I don't like it."

"Whatever. You still shouldn't kill Wolf when you get your hands on him."

"What would you suggest I do with him, then?" I ask, watching her closely.

"Hold him hostage," she says and I have to admit, she shocks the hell out of me with that answer.

"Hold him hostage?" I laugh.

"Yep," she says, shaking her head firmly once, as if to back up her words.

"Ice, who in the fuck am I going to hold him hostage for? No one is going to pay to save this sorry piece of shit."

"Oh my God, Liam! I don't remember you being so dense when we were together. *I'm saying* that you should capture him, put a big red bow on him, then give him to Devil as a Christmas present."

"I can't...*A Christmas present?*"

"Yes, a very much alive one."

"Ellie—"

"That's one gift that I know Devil will love."

"You get that if I do that, Devil's just going to kill him, Ice? You won't be saving his life."

"Gee, you think? I didn't say he didn't need to die. I just think that if he does, it should be Devil's right to do the deed."

"You're sounding awful blood-thirsty for a woman who ended our marriage because I left to kill someone, Ice," I mumble, confused as hell, admitting to myself that she's right about what I should do with Wolf. Diesel means well, but in this…*he's wrong.*

"You weren't going to just kill anyone, Liam. You were going to end the life of Ryan's mother. That's a completely different situation."

"She still needed to die, Ice."

"I can't agree with you on that."

"Remind me to tell you what that bitch did to Ryan and Rory someday soon, Ice."

"You can, but it won't change my opinion. She might have been crap, but she was still Ryan's mother. She deserved the chance to pull her life together and be a good Mom to her son. The court would have given Diesel custody…"

"Diesel had custody, Ice. But someone that's evil clean through is nothing but a starved animal, searching for something to fill their emptiness. They don't pay attention to rules and laws. You're dreaming if you think they do."

"I don't think it will ever happen, but what if I fell victim to addiction, Liam? Would you end me to protect our child?"

"That would never happen, Ice, and you know it. You're too strong to let addiction rule your world."

"Addiction can happen to anyone. Play devil's advocate for a minute. Tell me what you would do."

"You really want to do this shit right now?" I ask her, annoyed at her line of questioning. It's stupid. I really don't want to waste my time on this shit. I'd rather spend it enjoying her.

"I want to know. What would you do?"

"Fine, I'd lock your ass in rehab until you got clean. If you refused to go, I'd lock you in the basement and fight your withdrawals with you. Either way, I'd get you back, Ice. It's a moot point, however, because you're not addicted to anything but my dick. Now, let's move on."

"You mean that, don't you? You'd stay by my side, even with that between us."

"Ellie, I told you nothing can separate us, but you."

"I've been so stupid..."

"Ellie..."

"What you do, the things you're called on to do, Liam...they *still* scare the crap out of me."

"Ellie—"

"*But*, I've been without you all this time and I've been miserable. I didn't even know how miserable until you showed up and I was around you again."

"Ellie—"

"I was wrong, Liam. I should have waited and talked with you. I should have given us a chance to work through my fears and I didn't..."

"Does this mean you're coming back to me, Ellie?" I ask her, my heart squeezing tightly in my chest. I need her to say yes. I'm not letting her get away from me again, but it sure as hell would make things a lot easier if she admits she belongs with me sooner rather than later.

"There are still things we need to work through. Can we take time to do that? You'll be here in Arizona anyway, right? Can you give that to me, Liam?"

I hold the side of her face, bending down until our noses are touching. I close my eyes and calm my thoughts.

"I'm here for as long as it takes to prove to you that you belong home in Tennessee with me."

"Liam?"

"Yeah, baby?"

"I'm going to kiss you now. I'm not giving you a choice, more of a heads up," she murmurs, and I laugh.

In the end, we meet each other for the kiss.

ELLIE

"Slush, can you get that carton I left on the dolly in my office?" I ask the new daytime bartender. He's a good kid. Definitely a kid. I mean, I'm not over the hill by a longshot, but he's barely old enough to serve. His name is Billy, but for some reason he insists everyone call him Slush or Slushie. I shake my head again at just the thought.

Maybe I am older than I want to admit.

"Sure thing, ma'am."

I close my eyes. *Oh my God! ma'am?* I am old.

"Darn it," grumble under my breath. It wasn't that long ago I was making boys like him beg for my attention," I grumble under my breath.

"You don't need a boy, you need a man."

My gaze immediately jerks to the man that just sat at the bar. I don't know him, and yet there seems something familiar about him. He's older, much older than me. If I had to guess, I'd say late forties, maybe even early fifties. He wears it well. He has black hair that is slightly long. It's a jet black which might not be natural, but is appealing. He also has a goatee, which I always thought were weird, but on him, it's a good look.

"Sorry, I didn't realize we had a customer. It's usually pretty quiet in here the first hour we're open."

"Don't apologize. I'm enjoying the view," he says and his grin borders on lecherous. He thinks he's being flirty. With his looks, I'd imagine it works for him often. It doesn't work on me, however. I'd like to say it's because I have Liam in my life again, but the truth is something about this guy spells bad news and not in a hot night and regrets in the morning kind of way.

I jump down off the step ladder, wiping my hands on the cut-off jeans that I'm wearing.

"What can I get you to drink?"

"Will you have a drink with me?" he asks, his eyes darkening so much that they cause chills to run over me and again...*they're not the good kind.*

"Sorry, don't drink while at work."

"All business and no pleasure?" he asks and there goes those warning bells inside my head again. I can't say why this particular man seems to trip every alarm I have, but he does.

"What can I get you to drink?" I ask again, ignoring his flirting.

"Beer, house tap is fine."

I grab the one of the glasses we keep chilled, fill it up, sliding it over to him with a fake smile.

"What's your name?" he asks.

"Why do you ask?"

"Because you're beautiful and I want to know. I really don't want to call you ma'am either."

"That I'd appreciate," I respond, trying to let my guard down a little—not much, but as manager, I'm supposed to be friendly with the patrons. The last thing I need is for someone to file a complaint against me with Harvey. I don't think he'd listen to them, but with Harvey it's always better to be safe rather than sorry.

"So, your name?"

"Where you want these, Ellie? Slush asks, giving the guy my

name. I don't know what I would have said to the man, but for some reason, I don't like him having my name. Maybe I've had too much caffeine this morning and just being silly.

"Ellie, is that short for something?" the guy asks. If nothing else, I could definitely give him points for persistence.

"I'm just Ellie," I shrug, more or less lying, but it doesn't matter. "Slush help me get these boxes around the bar and I'll unpack while you take over."

"You got it."

"Ellie is a pretty name, but you look kind of exotic. You deserve a name to match. Your parents did you a great injustice."

"You don't know my parents. I'm just glad I didn't end up with a name like Andromeda."

"They were into Greek mythology?" he asks and I blink.

"Um...no. Geeky, Sci-Fi television shows," I respond. For some reason, he laughs. The laugh feels fake, much like everything about him.

"How about you go out with me tonight, Ellie?"

"Sorry, I don't date customers," I tell him at once.

"I haven't taken a drink of my beer yet. We can throw it away, that way I wouldn't be a customer."

"It still wouldn't work," I tell him. "I'm kind of seeing someone."

It feels weird to think of Liam like that. I mean it's not wrong. I woke up curled into him this morning. We're not having sex, but we're spending a lot of time together. We're falling into old habits, which to be honest, I missed more than I realized. I'm laughing more and so is he. It's early and he doesn't know... everything, but it feels like we're finding our way back to each other. Some things haven't changed, but maybe my outlook has. I shrug away the thoughts. I'll think about all of it later. I can only take things day by day right now and that's what Liam asked me to do. This is important and I can't let my fears keep me from trying.

"I didn't figure a pretty thing like you would be single. But, maybe I could show you I'm a better option."

"Well, I can say that modesty is not your problem," I laugh.

"If I don't know my worth, who will?" he says with a grin, but I got a feeling he's not really joking. Still, I guess he's not wrong. His is however, arrogant as hell. He reeks of it.

"I'm guessing everyone will know, because you're the type to tell them," I respond, studying him closely for the first time and trying to figure out why he makes me feel so uneasy.

"You make that sound like a bad thing, Ellie."

"Not always."

"But sometimes?" he prompts.

I wish I could figure out why he looks familiar. I can't. I'm still certain I don't know him, however. I guess it's possible he's been in here before. He's wearing jeans and a faded t-shirt. It's an INXS shirt, so he's into rock music, I guess. I never liked the band, but that's a personal choice, I guess. Plenty did.

"Hey, El? You got a phone call," Trina calls from out back.

Saved by the bell.

"Excuse me for a minute," I tell the strange customer, picking up the phone.

"Charlie, you can call me Charlie, Ellie. Our names kind of rhyme. Maybe that's fate."

"Charlie..." I repeat.

"You don't like the name?"

"No, it's a good name." *It is.* Liam hates it, but that's because his first name is Charlie and he loathes it. "My ex-husband's name was Charlie."

"Don't hold that against me. Maybe you just got the wrong Charlie the first time around," he says. Then, he puts down a fifty-dollar bill beside his untouched beer. "Be seeing you around, Ellie."

"Hello?" I hear Fury growling through the phone, pulling my attention away from the man leaving the bar.

"Hey, Liam."

"What was that shit about?"

"What shit?"

"Why are you talking about my first name, Ice?"

"Some customer said his name was Charlie and I just told him my ex-husband's name was the same. Geez, did Captain grouchy pants forget his coffee this morning?" I mumble, walking from behind the bar toward my office. "Holler if you need me, Slush."

"Yes, ma'am," he responds and I cringe.

"Liam, am I old?"

"What?"

"This new kid keeps calling me ma'am."

"Ice," he growls.

"I'm serious, Liam. It's freaking me out."

"Christ, woman, you're not even thirty."

"I know, but it's out there, floating around, waiting to drown me."

"I can't deal with this bullshit right now. I want to know why you were telling some fucker I'm your ex-husband."

"Because you are. Liam, please focus here. *He called me ma'am!*"

"I told you I'd remedy that shit. You want a paper, I'll come pick you up now. We'll get you a fucking paper."

"That's not how this is done."

"Seems to me it is."

I breathe a heavy, annoyed sigh into the phone. "When I drown because I'm old, shriveled and thirty, will you still be this annoying?"

"If you drown, I'll give you mouth to mouth. No more telling loser-assholes that I'm your ex. I'm your man, period."

"You're my ex and *maybe* my man," I argue, knowing I'm even kind of lying, but enjoying arguing with him. "Besides how do you know he's a loser? He could have been a really nice guy."

"He's at a bar hitting on a woman who belongs to someone else at ten-thirty in the fucking morning. He's a loser."

Okay, it should be said that Liam is kind of smart in an annoying, bossy as heck, kind of way. I ignore that, choosing to concentrate on the other part of what he said.

"Belongs to someone else? You make me sound like an old bag you pack your workout gear in and take to the gym," I mumble.

"I can give you a workout if you want," he says, his voice deepening in pleasure.

"Tell me why I like you again."

"My big dick?"

"Liam!"

"You going to deny it, Ice?"

"Please tell me you're not standing in the middle of the church right now?"

"What would it matter? God knows he gave me a big dick and he knows you like it, too."

"I may kill you."

"You remember the way you used to cry out and moan when I'd fuck you, Ellie? *Everyone* knew you liked my dick."

I squirm in my seat, trying to ignore the way his words make my panties wet and my nipples harden. The problem is I do remember and God, I miss him.

"You're impossible."

"I'm horny, I need you."

"You said you were going to give me time, Liam," I remind him, closing my eyes because I want him just as badly.

"I will, but doesn't change the truth. I need you, Ice."

"I need you, too. I just…" I break off, because I don't know what to say, I just know that taking the next step with him scares me.

"That's enough… *for now*."

I sigh. There's so much I could say—so much I should *probably* say. But, I don't. Instead, I change the subject because that seems safer for now.

"I take it that Wolf didn't show up this morning?"

"Not so far, no. I don't want to leave yet, though. I was just checking on you."

Warmth fills me. "I'm good, Liam."

"Yeah, you are," he purrs quietly, making the warmth inside of me intensify.

What am I waiting for?

"Can you take a lunchbreak?" I ask.

"It's probably not smart."

"I could bring lunch to you. We could eat outside on one of the tables in the church yard, or if you need to be more covert—"

"Covert," he laughs and I grin into the phone.

"We can eat in my vehicle."

"I'll take that, even though I shouldn't. I want to see you, Ellie."

"I'll be there around one."

"Sounds good, baby," he says, his voice soft, as then he ends the call. I hold the phone for a little bit longer.

And I do it smiling.

FURY

*I*t's almost nine. I've been outside church, along the tree line, so I could keep the perimeter in my eyesight at all times. I'm tired, hungry and cold. I also have no clue where Wolf is, because he didn't show today.

I've been careful, so I don't think he had a chance to see me. I doubt I have him spooked in any way. Hell, even when I took lunch with Ellie, I had her park in the parking lot across the street from the church. I could still see the church like that, but kept her away enough that hopefully Wolf wouldn't see her. The last thing I need is for that fucker to get her in his sights. I thought for sure the bastard would have shown up today, though. He's not one to just take the Sister's no and move along. He would come back in to investigate. There's security on the church, so if he tries to break in tonight, the police will be alerted. I have Scorpion back home keeping an eye out for any break-ins here. It's shitty that I'm not doing it myself, since I'm closer, but I wanted time with Ellie. Besides, considering she's all I could think about this last hour, I'm useless watching the church right now anyway.

When I walk in the house—using the key that Ice gave me this morning, the place is quiet. I kick off my boots, lock the door, and walk into the living room. Ellie is lying on the sofa. She's got a well-worn paperback in her hand, but she's not reading it. It's on the floor, because her hand has flopped down. Her blonde hair is secured on top of her head, but strands are going everywhere, pulled loose, ruffled from sleep.

It seems like a lifetime ago when I first fell in love with her. Being around her again has only made it clearer that I will always love her. I just need to convince her to fight for us. The truth is, I always expected Ellie to leave one day. She wasn't of my world. She didn't fully understand it. She pushed away any reservations she had just to be with me. I knew as much as she loved me, she wasn't one hundred percent in our relationship. Which meant, I prepared myself for her leaving since day one. Maybe that's the *real* reason I never tried going after her. I thought she'd be better off without me. Finding her again, seeing how much weight she's lost, the sadness in her eyes...I knew I was wrong. She might deserve better, but she's as twisted up in me as I am in her.

I walk over to the couch. Taking my cut off, I carefully lay it and the holster with my pistol on the end table. Then, I take her in my arms. "Fuck, Ice, you're warm."

"Liam?" she says while yawning, stretching against me as I pick her up. I settle on the couch, keeping her curled up in my lap.

"I forgot how you used to fall asleep reading, Ice. I've missed it."

"What time is it?"

"Almost nine," I tell her, leaning down to kiss the crinkle on her forehead.

"Are you hungry? I can heat you some of the leftover pizza," she mumbles.

"I grabbed something while I was out, Ice. You okay? No headache?"

"Nope. Not a sign of one in days. I hardly know how to act," she laughs, squeezing me as she wraps her arms around my waist.

"It's because I'm here with you," I reply with a grin, kissing the top of her head.

"You're so full of yourself, Liam," she laughs, but she doesn't deny it. "So, no Wolf."

"No Wolf," I mumble.

"Dag-nabbit."

I laugh, jostling her with my movements and shaking my head. "God, Ice."

"What?" she mutters, tilting her head to look up at me.

"You just make me happy, baby," I murmur. My words makes her face light up, all signs of sleep instantly gone. Maybe I should be cautious now, but I don't stop to think about it. I just bend down and kiss her.

Every kiss we share feels like the first one. It's always new. This one is no different. It's slow, but just as intense. Our tongues dance with one another, slowly remembering things forgotten, reacquainting each other with things we've missed, and discovering the new. I lose myself in the kiss, in her—just like I always do.

Slowly, my hand moves down to her breast. I stop there, half expecting her to stop me, but to my surprise, she doesn't. If anything, she deepens the kiss, pressing against me, silently asking for more. I knead her breast, brushing my thumb against the taunt nipple, feeling it grow even harder. Her fingernails bite into my back, our mouths getting more desperate to taste each other. A kiss that started off slow, is now becoming intense, hurried and full of need.

I feel her hand tunnel under my shirt, her fingers sliding against the top of my jeans. We break apart, dragging air into our lungs, I kiss along the side of her neck, raking my teeth against the sensitive skin and then sucking it in my mouth, tasting it, marking it. She angles her head, offering it to me, and satisfaction slams through me.

"You're playing with fire, Ice," I warn her, my voice low and hoarse with the hunger I feel for her.

"I want to. It's been so long, Liam. I want to feel you inside of me again," she whispers so softly that I have to concentrate to hear what she's saying, but the minute I do, it's as if the words wrap around my dick. I'm so hard that it's painful.

"You need to be sure, Ellie. I'm hanging on by a thread here, baby."

"Then stop and help me to get your pants undone," she demands, lifting her head to look at me. The minute she does, I see the need on her face, and I'm lost.

I hope to God she doesn't have regrets, because I'm claiming my woman and once I do...

She will never get away from me again.

ELLIE

 L iam lays me down on the sofa, standing over me, his gray eyes boring into me. *God, I've missed this.* The intensity in him as he's about to take me always makes me feel like the most desirable woman on the face of the earth. I lean up on my elbows, licking my lips, wanting him more than I can ever remember wanting him before.

"Take that fucking shirt off, Ice," he orders, his voice this low, smoke-filled tone that sends shivers all over my body. *Another thing I've missed.* Liam was always in control in the bedroom. He ordered and I obeyed without question. I trusted him to take me to a place that was nothing but pleasure and he never failed. *Not once.*

My hands shake as I lift the bottom of my shirt up and yank it over my head. I'm not scared, I'm that hungry for him.

"Now the bra."

I swallow, wondering if I am going to come before he even touches me. As I undo my bra, dropping it to the floor, it's a near miss.

"That's my good girl. I've missed those tits, Ice."

i

I start smiling without realizing it. I look up at him as a small laugh escapes.

"Just the tits?"

"You know better than that," he replies, pulling his gaze up to look at my face. Slowly he lowers to his knees in front of me. My breath stalls in my chest, suddenly this moment feels so much bigger, more momentous. I know in my heart it's because this is the first step. We go through with this and I'm taking Liam back into my life. We're going to try to put the past behind us. Even though I know that this is what I want, I can't help but be nervous. "Offer yourself to me, Ellie."

My eyelids get heavy as desire pushes through me with the force of a hurricane. I move my hands down to cup the under-swell of my breasts and hold them out to my man.

My man. That's what he is. That's what he's always been. I've always been his. From the moment I first looked up to find him staring at me, I've belonged to Liam.

I stop thinking when his lips brush against my nipple, a small whimper escaping me as I close my eyes and prepare for the plea-sure that only he can give me. Without warning his mouth clamps down on my nipple, sucking it inside his mouth. He doesn't try to be soft and seductive. Instead my Liam is harsh, rough, powerful and almost extreme. But, that's exactly how I like it. I love every minute of it.

"Fuck, yeah," he growls, his hands urgently fumbling with my pants. "Need you naked, Ice. I'm going to eat out your cunt. We'll see if it's as sweet as I remember. Then, if you're a good girl I'll make you gag on my fucking cock."

My hands join his, wanting out of my pants as much as he wants me out of them. Liam rarely does sweet talk in bed. He's crass and demanding. It's always made it more exciting. It calls to the darkness inside of me that loves being dominated.

He yanks my pants down, taking my panties with them. He doesn't move and I'm desperate for something from him. I look at him, ready to beg him to do more, but I stop because he's looking down at my pussy in a way I haven't seen from him before.

"Liam?" I ask, softly almost afraid.

"Dreamed, Ice."

"What?"

"I've fucking dreamed for almost two years of having you back, of looking down at your body, of seeing your sweet cunt wet and glistening, ready to be fucked. You've haunted me, Ellie."

"Liam," I murmur, brokenly, because his voice is raw and there's no doubting the sincerity of it.

"You're not taking it away again. You're not leaving me again," he says and this time when he looks at me, there's a fire raging behind his gaze. It's burning so strong that I can feel the heat from it. "These are mine." He reaches out and brushes his calloused finger over my swollen nipples as he says that, his voice guttural. He leans down, kissing each nipple. It's just a small kiss, but I can still feel the emotion behind the action. I'm so wet that I shiver as the cool air of the room hits the wetness between my legs. Whatever comes next, I know that when Liam finally lets me come, it will be so intense that I may not survive. "This is mine," he adds, that same finger sliding against my lips. We stare at each other as I open my mouth, taking his finger inside and sucking on it like it was his cock. For a mere moment, his eyes close and his strong, demanding body shudders.

I did that.

He wants me so much that I make him burn. I love that more than I could ever explain. I've always felt it was a gift that Liam reacts like that to me...*with* me. To see that it hasn't changed, despite us being apart, feels like a miracle.

His hand slides down between my legs, his fingers dragging along the lips of my pussy, gathering the wetness that has collected there.

"Liam...," I gasp, as his fingers slip and press inside, before slowly moving to caress my clit. He's teasing me, but not entering where I need them the most.

"So wet and fucking ready and I've not even tried to get you there, yet," he groans.

"I need you," I respond, simply.

"This is mine," he grunts, his fingers pushing hard against my throbbing clit. His entire hand is holding my pussy tightly. It's a rough possession that makes me even wetter.

"Liam," I cry, my body trembling with need.

"Tell me, Ellie. Tell me what I need to hear."

"It's all yours, Liam. *I'm* yours."

His lips press against mine then, taking any other words I might say, his tongue thrusting inside to ravage. It's almost violent, our teeth clashing, our tongues fighting and breath coming through in desperation.

He stands up and through desire-filled eyes, I watch as he undoes his pants, pushing them down his long, muscular legs. His cock, fully erect, wide, long, and throbbing, springs outward. It's curved slightly to one side, the head shiny, wet and dark. I watch as he takes it in his hand and grabs the shaft tightly.

"I'm going to fuck you so hard you're not going to be able to walk tomorrow, Ice," he vows. In answer, I spread my legs open for him.

I'm on a razor's edge, desperate for more. He jerks his head up, taking his attention from me. At first, I'm confused. Then, I hear the door open from the other room.

"What the fuck. I locked the door," he growls. He reaches down and kicks his pants off, swiftly reaching over to the end table. He grabs his cut, throwing it over me. Then, he's holding a pistol he must have hidden there. "Keep covered and don't move, Ice," he hisses. He aims his gun, taking a couple of steps toward the kitchen, his dick swinging with each step. If I wasn't terrified, I'd have to laugh.

And then, I hear the voices and I want to kill...

"I don't want to fight about it anymore, Dawn. I told you what I want and you need to figure shit out. You knew what I liked before we got together."

"Don't you tell me that shit. I thought I was what you fucking wanted when we got together," my sister growls.

Yep, definitely going to kill them.

I know Liam knows who is there now, because he's not as tense and the vibe coming off of him is not as deadly. He still doesn't withdraw his gun, however. That could be a problem, because he's never liked Dawn—or my mother really. He never liked how they treated me and he used to insist that something about Dawn felt...*off*. I've tried to convince him that Dawn is just an acquired taste, but he always just gave me a look, and changed the subject.

"I do want you. I just like guys too. You knew that, so you can't act like a little bitch when I want to play. I'm including you. It's not like I'm going out and fucking an entire football team behind your back, for fuck's sake."

"You invited him without asking me first, you slut-bag. That's *why* I'm pissed. If we're in a relationship—" Dawn stops talking when she looks up and sees a naked-below-the-waist Liam pointing a gun at her and Glenna. "What in the *fuck* are you doing here?" she snarls.

Hate comes off of her in waves. Dawn has never been one of Liam's biggest fans either. That only got worse when I came home, grieving while waiting for Liam to call—only to never hear from him.

"Ding-fucking-Dong. Meat Show alert," Glenna literally purrs. I grab Liam's cut and put it on, covering my breasts. I reach down, getting my panties. I put them on so quick that I am almost dizzy. "Fuck. Do you see, Dawn? *That's* what we're missing. It has to be at least twelve inches...or more."

"If I wanted dick, I wouldn't have tossed Colin aside for you," Dawn huffs. I go and stand in front of my man, because I don't want anyone seeing Liam's dick but me. "What the hell are you doing here, Ape Hanger?" Dawn snarls.

I can feel Liam's body tighten with anger behind me. Because my sister never liked Liam, she insisted on calling him that to make fun of the bike he was riding the first time she met him.

"Ape Hanger? Shit. He's more like the Bone Ranger and suddenly I want to be Tonto," Glenna chimes in.

"Ice," Liam mutters, his free hand coming down on my shoulder. I can hear his annoyance, but it's nothing compared to mine.

I'm going to kill Dawn...

ELLIE

"*W*here's Shit-For-Brains?"

"Dawn, will you stop?"

"Ellie, will you grow a brain? What are you doing letting that asshole near you again? Didn't you learn the first time he broke your heart?" Dawn snaps and I sigh. I knew this wasn't going to go easy. It's one of the reasons I purposely didn't tell her or Mom that I was talking to Liam again. Dawn might be older than me by a few years, but most times she acts like she's thirteen and never going to grow up.

"I left him, remember?"

"Because you didn't have a choice. You always were so weak when it came to that shit. You have to be strong. This world doesn't owe you anything and the last thing you should ever do is let people run over you."

"I'm not weak. I had choices," I mumble, because I did and I'm starting to think I made the wrong one.

"Whatever. You always let people run over you. Besides, you wouldn't tell me why you left—"

"That's because it was no one's business. It was between me and Liam, no one else," I insist, stubbornly. It was really between the club and Liam, but even though I was upset with the things that Liam was put in charge of, I would never betray his confidence in me.

"You say that, but it was me and Mom who put you back together and helped you stand after he left you miserable."

"He didn't leave me!" I yell. "I left and I'm starting to think maybe I shouldn't have. I think maybe I made a mistake, Dawn."

"You're just saying that because you want laid. I'm so sick of women who can't even think straight when they get near a man's dick. What is so great about those damn things, anyway? They're ugly as hell. They look like a mushroom that was outside during a nuclear explosion."

"Will you give it a rest? Would you like to know what I think about vaginas? Even the name alone is gross," I respond and get instantly rewarded with what I like to call her scrunched-up-bitch-face.

"You need to kick his ass to the curb."

"My relationship with Liam is my business. Lay off of him. We have problems, but we're trying and I may not know a lot, but I know that Liam is the only man I'll ever love."

"Whatever," she sighs and I notice she's staring at the stairs and looking unsure of herself. I'm not used to that from Dawn. Hell, most of the time she scares me. Dawn is headstrong, loud and stubborn. She never backs down and there's always a seething anger inside of her. Mom has traces of it, but Dawn is definitely more extreme.

I follow her gaze up the stairs. Glenna went up there to the guest bedroom not long after they got here. Liam is upstairs in my bed, giving me time with my sister. He kissed me good night and gave Dawn a goodbye that sounded more like an undistinguishable grunt. He should probably get sainthood for that, considering how she acts towards him and exactly what Dawn interrupted.

"You want to tell me what's going on with you and Glenna?"

"Nothing," she mumbles.

"Now who is lying?"

"She told me on the way down here tonight that she doesn't want to be in a committed relationship with me anymore."

"Shit."

"Yeah. What really sucks, is that what she really means is she wants to start dating guys again. I mean I get it, she likes both men and women. She's always been upfront with me about that. But, she promised me when we started seeing each other that I was enough. She swore she was happy. Now, barely two months in..."

"I'm sorry, Dawn."

"It doesn't matter. I'll handle it."

"Have you tried talking to her and letting her know that —"

"Save it, Sis. I've had this conversation. Her compromise is she wants to have a threesome partner."

"How do you feel about that?"

"I'll talk to you in the morning," she grumbles, shutting down the conversation.

"Okay."

"Will you do me one favor?"

"What's that?"

"Be careful with that asshole. He fucked you over. If someone does that shit, you don't give them a chance to do it twice, Ellie. No matter what."

I swallow, memories of what I went through and the pain of losing...*everything*, threaten to crash in on me. I shake it off and do my best to give her a reassuring smile.

"I promise, I'm being careful."

She nods once. "Does he know?"

"Not everything, no."

"Are you going to tell him?" she asks, studying me closely.

"I'm not sure. There's nothing either of us can do to change the past now," I tell her and she gives me a sad smile.

"Tread carefully, Ellie. Liam isn't exactly the most forgiving of men."

My stomach clenches at her words, but I do my best to act like I'm not worried. I'm not sure she buys it. I didn't tell Dawn everything, but I told her enough.

She goes upstairs to face her own problems, though, leaving me alone with mine. Suddenly, a night that had so much promise has fallen flat.

ELLIE

"You get shit lined out?" Liam asks, when I make it upstairs. I stop at the door and look at him lying on my bed. He doesn't have a shirt on, and I'd lay odds that he's naked under those covers. His dark hair is ruffled and stands out against my white pillow cases and sheets. The ice blue comforter is pulled up to his hip and lazily hides all of his goodies. That thought makes me grin. "Ellie?" he prompts, and I can hear the worry in his voice. He's worried about me.

That feels nice.

"They went to bed. I think they're still arguing, I could hear traces of it as I passed their door, but at least they're not screaming."

"Your sister is a fucking mess, Ice."

I'm wearing Liam's shirt he had on earlier and I decide it's perfect to sleep in. I just want to lie in bed and cuddle up to my man. I walk over to him, slide under the covers and immediately he pulls me into his warm body, his arm going around me, my head resting on his chest.

"She's hurting, Liam."

"I get that, Ice, which shocks the fuck out of me. I didn't think the bitch had a heart."

"Liam—"

This shit won't get any better the way she's going at it."

"You don't like her," I mutter, they've always fought with each other and it's definitely made it hard in the past. I don't know why I thought it would have changed after all of this time. When I left Liam and he didn't come and find me, Dawn's anger toward him grew, so I should have known better.

"I've always told you there's something about her I don't trust. Still, she cares about you. She's got grit and she doesn't take shit— at least in life. I can respect her for that."

I look up at him, surprised. "You mean that?"

"Yeah, baby. We butt heads, yet we both care about you. I can live with that. She wants you cared for and respected. The problem is with her. Right now, she's not demanding that same respect from the people she's trying to let into her life. That is a fucking recipe for disaster.

Liam is not wrong. My sister goes through relationships like water. She's never really treated any of them that great. Things were different with Glenna, however. She seems to really care for her. She seemed really happy for once, so to see them fighting now makes me hurt for her.

"She's going to agree to bring another person into their relationship."

"Dawn's okay with that?" Liam asks, his fingers rubbing against my temple, stroking my hair.

"I don't think so. I think she's doing it so she doesn't lose Glenna."

"She'll definitely lose her then," Liam predicts and it makes me sad, because I'm afraid he's right.

"Maybe not? Maybe bringing a man into the bedroom will—"

"Ice, it's hard enough being a couple in this world. You bring a third party into the bedroom, then you better be solidly committed to each other, because feelings and emotions can trip a motherfucker up."

"Why does it sound like you know all about this?" I ask, not liking the idea at all.

"I don't, at least not personally. I got a buddy that I served overseas with and he was tight with this other dude, Sabre. I didn't know Sabre as well, but he seemed like a good enough guy. Sabre brought my guy into the relationship he had with his wife."

"It didn't work?"

"Worked really good. The three of them seemed extremely happy. Annie is a sweet woman and Latch? He needed that. He hadn't had that shit in his life."

"Then, I don't—"

"He fell in love with Annie."

"So? I mean you said they were happy together. He and Sabre obviously had to love each other. It sounds like the perfect situation. Unless, Annie didn't care—"

"I don't think I've met one person that Annie doesn't care for. She's a good woman with a big heart, Ice."

"Then, I don't understand."

"Latch and Sabre respect each other, they're brothers in every sense of the word except by blood, but they don't get off on each other's dicks. Their threesome is all about Annie and giving her pleasure."

"Oh, wow. That's kind of amazing if you think about it. Annie's a lucky woman."

"That something you want, Ice?"

"What?" I gasp, my face heating, because I was imagining being a woman that had two men in her bed, focused completely on me. It seems like the ultimate fantasy. I don't think it's something I could do, but I can see the appeal.

"Fuck, you do," Liam says, as he tilts his face down to look at me.

"Liam—"

"You want that, Ice. I'll give it to you."

"You would?" I ask, completely shocked. There are many things I know about Liam in the bedroom, but none of those screams that he shares well with others. I've always kind of liked that. This is a revelation and I'm not sure how I feel about it. I'm a little excited, maybe even scared, but weirdly disappointed, too. Mostly, I'm overwhelmingly confused.

Definitely confused.

"I love you, Ellie. If you want that, then I'm going to give it to you, but it will be on my terms."

"Your terms?"

"I pick the man. It has to be someone I trust, implicitly. Also, I control what happens and it only happens in a hotel, not our bed. Our bed is *ours*. You and me. I don't want to be fucking you and some other fucker be there, *ever*."

I pull back to listen to Liam, and watch him as he lays it out. I don't know how I feel about it, but I can tell he's got very clear feelings about everything and I want to watch his face. I prop my head up on my hand, my elbow pushing into the mattress.

"What else," I murmur, sifting through everything he says, while trying to wrap my mind around the fact that Liam is saying all of this. I mean I was married to him. We were together for a while and yet, this completely shocks me.

"His dick never gets inside of you. You have a baby, it's mine. I come inside of you, it's my cum. I don't want some fucker's there hanging out before me."

"I uh...I'm not sure that's how it works. The just hanging out inside of me thing, because...eww."

"I'm serious, Ellie."

"I can see that," I whisper, because I can. Actually, he's getting kind of worked up about it the more he talks, and not in good ways. He seems...*upset*. Heck, he might even be pissed off. "What about my mouth?" I ask, knowing I'm poking the bear at this point, but I need to see where this goes.

"Fuck, no," he growls. "You never suck another motherfucker off. I'm not kissing my woman only to taste some other man's jizz. That's never happening," he declares absolutely. "I've made it all this time without tasting some ball bag's cum and I'm not changing that now."

"I…okay, so let me get this straight. You'll give me a threesome, but the guy isn't allowed to actually…*do* me and I can't get him off, do I have that right?"

"He can touch you, but only when and how I tell him," Liam allows. "And you can use your hand on him, but only if you want to. He has to have a condom though. His cum is not allowed to touch your body."

I let out a startled laugh.

"What?" Liam asks, defensively.

"It doesn't sound like much fun for him, Liam. I doubt you can find a man to agree."

"Bullshit. He gets to touch you and see you come, Ellie. Trust me, finding someone who wants that is the easy part."

It's a weird compliment, but a compliment all the same. It makes me lean up and kiss the tip of Liam's chin—mostly because that's all I can reach from this angle. Then, a thought occurs to me and I frown.

"Would you want that?" I ask.

"What?"

"Would you want me to bring another woman into our relationship, because I have to tell you, Liam, I don't think I could handle that at all. I don't want another woman anywhere near you. *Ever.*"

I watch as his lips slowly stretch out into a sexy smile and if I wasn't terrified of the fact that he could possibly want another woman in our bed, I'd definitely enjoy that smile and try to keep it on his face.

"Fuck, no, Ice. You're the only woman I want. I haven't wanted anyone else since the day I first saw you," he says softly, his hand coming to my neck, as his thumb brushes against my pulse. His gray eyes go dark and intense and my entire body tingles. Heck, I think even my toes curl.

"I don't think I want another man in our relationship either, Liam. It's a good fantasy, but the reality of it doesn't really appeal to me," I confess. "You were my first and I'm praying this works out so that you'll be the last."

"Ellie," he hisses, leaning down to take my mouth. This kiss is different than the others we've shared since he came back into my life. This kiss is sweet and slow, thoughtful, and reminds me of the kiss he gave me on our wedding day.

Full of love.

When we break apart, he settles me back against him, reaches over and turns out the light. We lie there in the darkness for a bit and I go over everything we just talked about.

"We could finish what we started earlier, if you wanted," I offer him, knowing he has to have a case of blue balls. I hate that we got interrupted.

"Your head is full of worry over your sister, Ice. I think I could pull you out of that, but I'd rather our first time back with each other was because we're both where we need to be emotionally *and* mentally."

"Whatever happened to Latch?"

"He went back into service for a while. It hurt him to be in love with Annie, but only be able to see her when they asked him."

"Are they still together?"

"Last I heard, yeah, but Annie's pregnant with her second child. I'm not sure Latch is dealing with that all that well. Maybe they've sorted it out by now, I don't know. I haven't talked to him in a couple of months. I just know my man was seriously nursing a broken heart, even still being in their lives."

"That's sad," I whisper, feeling my heart hurt for Latch.

"That's why rules for bringing another person into a

committed relationship need to be stated. It's most definitely why, a couple needs to be solid to even entertain the idea."

"Do you think it can work?"

"Yeah, I think so."

"But, you don't think it will work for Dawn," I murmur, my voice laced with sadness. I had hoped this was a turning point for my sister. I don't want to say she's been selfish in her life, but she's definitely the type of person to put herself first. Sometimes that's not bad, but all the time?

"No, Ice, I don't. This isn't something that both of them want. This is something she's doing to try and save her relationship."

"Which is also probably the quickest way to lose it, because Dawn will hate everything about it."

"She'll be okay, Ice."

"I'm not so sure," I murmur.

"I am."

"How?" I ask, hoping he can convince me.

"Because she has you and you will be there to pick up the pieces."

"You have a lot of faith in me, Liam," I mutter with a sad, exhausted sigh.

"All the faith in the world, Ellie. All the faith in the world."

He kisses the top of my head and I close my eyes feeling secure and loved. Liam and I have a lot to work out, but right now I feel nothing but hope and happiness when it comes to the two of us.

I pray that Dawn gets that feeling one day. *I really want that for her.*

FURY

 ne Week Later

"Hey, Ice."

"You don't look like you've had a good day, honey."

I slide onto the barstool, thinking her words might be the understatement of the century. She hands me a cold beer. It doesn't escape my attention that it's the brand I always drink. She remembers. Since having her back in my life, everything has just clicked into place. Does she realize that? Does she feel the same emotions that I feel?

"You can say that again," I mutter, twisting off the top, taking a deep pull.

"No sign of Wolf?"

"Not one. He could already be headed to Chicago," I mutter, frustrated because I was hoping to catch this motherfucker and finally giving Devil and Torrent some good news.

"But, if he didn't get the information from the church, he wouldn't know to do that, right?"

"Yeah, I guess so. It just doesn't make any sense that he would disappear."

"Maybe he's tired. You said it had been over a year. Maybe he just decided enough is enough," she suggests.

"He's not the type to give up. If he thought he could do something to cause trouble for Devil or Torrent, he'd move heaven and earth to do exactly that. He's as fucking twisted as they come."

"So, you think he's still in town."

"I'd bet good money on it," I reply.

"Well, if what you say is true, he'll show up again, Liam. You know that."

"Yeah, I do. That doesn't mean I like sitting around here, holding my damn dick in my hand. I hate waiting for this twisted asshole to make a move."

"I don't know," Ellie whispers, leaning in closer to me. "It doesn't sound so bad being stuck holding your dick in my hands."

Despite the stress and frustration of the day, I find myself grinning.

"You are a fucking tease, Eleanor Lane."

"Way to break the mood, Liam. You know I hate my first name."

"I love it. It makes you sound all prim and proper. We both know what a freak you can be in the bedroom."

"Uh...I'm not sure I'd use the word freak."

"I would."

"Jerk," she says, shaking her head and smiling at me. "Besides I wasn't teasing. We have the house alone tonight. I was thinking maybe we could pick up where we left off a week ago."

"You're kidding me."

"Nope, she's not," Dawn says sitting beside me and just like that my cock-stand begins to deflate.

"Dawn, where's your girl?"

"She's home packing our shit. Her and I are going away for the weekend."

"The whole weekend, huh?" I ask, enjoying the way Ellie blushes when I grin at her.

"That's right, so you can pork my sister all weekend, Ape Hanger."

"Didn't realize I needed your permission," I mutter, wondering how her and Ellie had the same parents because they're nothing alike.

"I guess you don't. Ellie makes up her own mind. If she listened to me she wouldn't give you the time of day."

"Dawn, don't start, please."

"Good thing she doesn't listen to you then. I don't want to fight with you, Dawn, but you need to get used to the fact that I'm back in Ellie's life and I'm not going anywhere."

"We'll see. It's not like you seem to have good staying power, Liam. After all, you disappeared when Ellie needed you most."

"Dawn," Ellie snaps, her tone full of warning and more forceful than I can remember her ever using. When I glance up at her face, she's staring straight at her sister and the irritation and anger is clear to read on her face.

"Relax, Ellie. Liam and I are just coming to an understanding. Am I right?"

"Yeah, you're right," I mumble.

"Good, now that we have that out of the way, I have a present for you, Liam," Dawn says.

"Now you're just fucking with me," I say with a dry laugh. I don't know what Dawn has up her sleeve, but I know her well enough to know that it's something to piss me off.

"Trust me, Liam, the last thing I ever want to do is fuck with you in any way, shape or form," she replies, setting a brown paper bag on the bar and shoving it towards me.

Reluctantly, I put my beer down with a thud against the bar and pick up the bag. The top has been rolled down and crinkled so I quickly open it. When I look inside I shake my damn head. I reach inside and grab a hand full of rubbers and put them on the bar. The size clearly states small and I shake my fucking head.

"You're a bitch, Dawn."

"If I had a dollar for every time someone said that to me. I'm not buying your damn condoms. You buy them for yourself, don't be a lazy fuck. If you want to pork my sister, then make sure you protect her, too. Do we understand each other?"

"We're crystal."

"Good. Now, I'm off to spend the weekend with Glenna and some fucking man with a dick that she met on Tinder."

"Christ, you're fucking kidding me," I growl.

"Don't act like you care, Ape Hanger."

"Believe it or not I do. You shouldn't do this shit if it's not what you want. Bitch needs to acknowledge she committed herself to you and that should be enough for her."

"Yeah, well, in a perfect world," Dawn mutters and Ellie puts a drink in front of her.

"I don't like this at all. I don't think you should do this, Dawn."

"Just let it go, Ellie. It's not like I'm enjoying all of it, either. Still, Glenna wants this and I love her."

Ellie and Dawn stare at each other and it feels like there's some nonverbal conversation passing between them.

"You need to be careful," Ellie cautions, apparently giving in.

"You got it, Mom," Dawn says, rolling her eyes.

"I want pictures, name and address of the man you're meeting and where you'll be, Dawn."

"Jesus, we're hooking up, I'm not marrying the motherfucker. If there's any luck, this weekend will show Glenna that she doesn't need a man to be happy."

"Just get me the information, please, especially a phone and address of where you'll be this weekend."

"Fine, I'll do it. Will you let it drop now?"

"For now," Ellie mutters and I reach out and grab her hand, giving it a squeeze. She stares at our hands, and there's something on her face that I can't read. I wish I could fix this so Dawn could finally be happy, but there's nothing I can do.

"What if you give me this guy's name and date of birth? I can at least get Scorpion to run a background check on him," I offer.

"Jesus, you two," Dawn growls. "It's a fucking hook up."

"Still, it's better to be safe rather than sorry, right?" Ellie says hopefully.

"I don't even know his date of birth," Dawn mumbles. "We'll be fine."

"Call and get it. If he's a good man, he won't mind that you're taking care of you and Glenna," I tell her, hoping she'll see the common sense in what I'm suggesting.

"You're both being ridiculous," she says, but she picks up the phone and I'm rewarded with the look of happiness on Ellie's eyes.

For some reason, I feel like I've won a war for her and it's a really damn good feeling.

ELLIE

"There's no sign of her?"

I listen as Liam talks to Scorpion on the phone. It sounds like things aren't going his way. I know he's getting frustrated and I'm afraid this means that he'll be forced to leave Arizona soon. I'm not sure I'm ready for that.

We've been playing house more or less. Living together, but not making love, ignoring the things that put the rift between us in the first place and, at least on my part, hiding from the past. I love Liam. I've always loved him and I know the time is fast approaching when I'm going to have to get my shit together. I'm either going back to Tennessee to try again, or let Liam know that I can't go back.

If I stay here, will he? Heck, even if he does, can I live with the fact that he chose me over the club? Once, that was all I wanted, but I knew the club was the only family he had ever known. He loves his brothers. Is it fair to ask him to give all of that up? Has anything really changed? What happens if he finds out my secret?

All I have are questions. My head probably knows the answers, but I'm scared of those, too.

"Okay, keep me updated, man. Yeah, and thanks again, Ellie will sleep easier knowing this shit. Whatever. I'll tell her. Later."

I listen to the one-sided conversation, then watch as he hangs up. I'm left staring at him. I mean, it's a great view. He's stretched out on my bed, lying with the cover over the lower half of his body. His hair is rumpled and he's reclined so that the headboard and pillows are at his back. He carefully tosses his phone onto the nightstand, staring at me. I feel a familiar chill of anticipation run through me, as our gazes lock. My breath quickens, while my heart stutters in my chest. Liam is back in my bed. He's really here, after all of this time.

"Does that mean, this guy checks out?" I reply and it's selfish, but the guy that Dawn and Glenna have found to join them in the bedroom is really the last thing I want to talk about. I'd rather concentrate on the fact that there's a miracle going on and Liam is back in my bedroom and I have a second chance. Things can be different this time. Can't they?

I hope I'm not fooling myself.

"Reginald "Reggie" Cleary is squeaky clean. He's never been married, has a great credit rating and no arrest record that Scorpion can find anywhere. He's a computer programmer and is based in Phoenix. He pays his taxes, as well as, his credit card bills. Scorpion says they all have extremely high charge limits, too. He checks out, Ice."

"That's something, I guess."

"It's a lot. What your sister is doing sucks for her, because I think she's going to end up on the short end of the stick, but as near as my guy can tell, this Reggie is safe and it could be a lot worse. You know?"

"I know," I murmur and I do. I'm just worried about Dawn, but at least now I'm not scared she's going to get herself killed. "Thank you for doing this, Liam. I know you didn't have to."

"Ice, I love you. Dawn may make me bat-shit crazy, but you

love her, so I'm going to do what I can to make sure she's taken care of, too. Family, you know?"

"Yeah, I do know. Your club is family and I was asking you to turn your back on them once."

"Ellie," he rumbles, ruffling his hair in frustration.

"I won't lie, Liam, it hurt the most that first year because it felt like you turned your back on me instead."

"You left me, Ice. You made your choices."

"And you didn't come after me. I sound like a bitch saying that, I know. I shouldn't have expected it. I didn't think I was playing a game by trying to make you run through hoops, but maybe I was. Maybe I wanted you to prove I mattered more than them," I tell him, wringing my hands, as I bare my heart to him.

"We both made mistakes, Ellie. I regret not coming after you, I do. But, things went south. It's not an excuse, but Vicki went into hiding, and I couldn't find her. She ambushed Diesel one day and tried to kidnap Ryan. She left Diesel for dead. Then, when things settled down, it just felt like so much time had passed. You hadn't called, and didn't answer when I called. I figured you were just done."

"We should probably talk about Vicki and the past and all the bullshit..."

"Fuck no. That's done. Diesel has Rory and he's happy. Ryan is loved and safe, things are good. The past needs to stay in the fucking past. You and I are going to concentrate on the future. I should have tried to find you when you didn't take my calls. That's on me. You shouldn't have left and tried to work this shit out, instead of bailing. That's on you. We both have fault, Ice. Now, we put this behind us and move forward, together."

"Liam... you didn't call me."

"I did, babe. I even spoke to your mom a couple of times."

"That's impossible. Liam. She would have told me. She knew how upset I was, what I was going through. She would have told me if you called."

"I can't explain that, Ellie. But you know I wouldn't lie to you."

"I need to call her…"

"Not right now. Right now, you need to come over here and take off your clothes."

"This is important, Liam," I mumble, even as my body trembles at the thought of undressing for him.

"This is more important. I told you the past is done. Now, come here."

My entire body trembles as his gray eyes seem to heat and turn molten as we look at each other. We've been doing this dance ever since Dawn interrupted us a week ago. Right now is decision time. There's no going back.

"Liam, I need to talk to you—"

"You need to get over here and offer yourself to me. The time for talking is over, Ice," he counters.

I swallow down my fear and walk over to him. He doesn't reach out to touch me, he doesn't do anything. *He just waits.* With trembling fingers, I slowly begin undoing my shirt.

"Lean down and give me your lips, Ice," he orders, his voice graveled and rough.

I stop undressing to do as he asks, holding onto his shoulders as I kiss him. The instant our lips touch, I forget everything else. He's right. Liam and I need to go forward. I can't change the past…no matter how much I wish I could.

ELLIE

"Strip," he orders as we break apart from our kiss.

The words seem to vibrate through me, causing my entire body to tremble.

I'm trembling like a lone leaf on a tree limb. This is important. I know it is. This is the beginning. There's so much we need to talk about—so much we need to work out. Making love with Liam might be the wrong move, but I can't make myself stop.

I take my clothes off in hurried, if not stilted, movements. I curse myself as I realize what I'm doing. I should be trying to be sexy, alluring. I should be flaunting what he's missed by not contacting me.

"Are you nervous, Ice?" he asks, watching me.

"Yes," I whisper, but that's not completely truthful. I *am* nervous, but I'm also violently turned on. I'm so wet that I can feel the moisture on the inside of my thighs. My nipples are painfully hard and just the cool air of the room makes me want to moan. It's been so long and Liam is the only one who has ever made me feel like this—like I'm the most desirable woman in the world.

He throws the cover off of his body revealing that he's completely naked. I bite my lip to stifle the moan that tries to escape. I watch as he moves his hand down and strokes his cock very slowly. I could watch him do that all day long. There's something so primal about the way his strong, inked hand moves over his huge cock, the head slick and wet and getting wetter with each stroke. The longer I watch, the more it feels like electricity moves through my body.

"You enjoying the show, Ice?"

"Definitely," I almost groan as one small pearl leaks from his dick and slides down against his hand. I long to lick that drop and claim it with my tongue.

"I've been thinking about this ever since I saw you again, Ellie."

"Me too," I admit.

"Please tell me you're on birth control, baby."

"I am, but…"

"I'm clean, Ice. Got a clean bill of health before heading out this way."

"Liam," I mumble, my brain mush. It shouldn't matter. He says he hadn't been with another woman. This is Liam. I let my worries go.

"Straddle me, Ice." I move to the bed, positioning myself over him, my knees pressing into the mattress. "Touch me, baby. I need your hands on me," he urges.

I immediately grip his hard cock. It's wet and the heavy veins seem to throb under my touch. I stroke him once, pre-cum sliding onto my fingers. Liam grabs my neck and pulls me down, his tongue pushing into my mouth with a hunger that matches mine. His tongue demands entry, devouring me. When the kiss ends, his eyes are filled with a need that the intense look on his face makes me grow even wetter.

"I hope you're ready," he growls, grabbing my hips.

"I am," I whisper.

"Then, take me inside," he says, holding me tightly.

I slide down on him, stopping about midway to catch my breath. It's been so long and he's so large that it's almost painful.

His hand reaches up to tease my nipples, giving me just what I need to slide down on him a little more and taking him in deeper. When I finally work him all the way in, I don't move. It takes a minute to get used to the full feeling and the way he stretches me. I can feel the walls of my pussy tremble around his cock, I squeeze tightly, moaning at how good that feels. Then, I slowly begin to ride him. It takes me a minute to find the rhythm to bring the most pleasure. I needn't worry, because soon Liam is taking over, using his hands on my hips to show me exactly what he wants. I rotate my hips on the downward thrust, because I love the way that makes the head of his cock rake against the walls of my pussy.

"Fuck, I forgot how good it feels to be inside of you, Ellie. There's nothing better," he moans. I put my hands on his chest, my nails biting into his skin, as I pick up my speed, riding him harder and faster now.

"Nothing...better," I gasp as I fuck myself on his cock. My breasts bounce as I ride him faster. I can feel my orgasm just beyond reach. I can feel the fierceness of it as it gathers. My pussy clamps tight on his cock as my climax crashes through me. I milk his cock, wanting everything he has to give me. He gives me his cum, and I moan because the force of his cum jetting inside of me feels like a physical touch it's so good. I collapse against his chest when it's over, his cum leaking down the side of my legs and I don't even care. I lay there, my head on his chest, his cock still buried deep inside of me and it's perfect.

ELLIE

"*He* got the all clear."

"So, I guess it's a go. I'll have Glenna call him tonight," Dawn replies, sounding anything but happy.

"There's still time for you to tell her that you don't want this and back out, Dawn," I caution her.

"Yeah and then, she will just go through with it without me."

"Let her, you'll find someone else."

"Like you did, Ellie?" she asks, her voice just a bit sarcastic, her remark bothering me. I breathe into the phone as I try to search for words.

"I love him."

"I love Glenna," she counters.

That pretty much says it all and I can't really argue with her. After all, Liam is asleep upstairs in my bed.

"Dawn, why didn't you and Mom tell me that Liam called me after I moved back home?" I ask softly. I expect her to deny it. It's not that I think Liam is lying to me, but if Dawn knew, she would tell me. We don't have secrets...or at least I didn't think we did. The longer she is silent, however, the more I begin to doubt that. My eyes close as this sense of betrayal fills me.

i

"That bastard had put you through enough. You were struggling."

"You don't think hearing from Liam might have helped me?"

"Or made it worse. You'd been home for a month, Ellie. He hadn't bothered to call you. That pretty much said everything we needed to know."

"He'd been out of town—"

"They don't have phones out of town?" Dawn snaps, and now her tone is defensive, but I don't want to hear it.

"You still should have told me," I murmur. "I've got to go. Be safe and check in."

"Ellie—"

"I can't right now, Dawn. Just promise to be safe and check in."

"Whatever," she says and I hang up.

I just stand there for a few minutes, staring at my cellphone, as I try and think about everything. All of this time, I thought I wasn't important to Liam. The fact that he called changes things. I can't go back, but it does matter just the same.

"Why don't you look like a woman whose man made her see stars last night?" Liam asks, and I jerk my head up.

"Called Dawn," I reply. The smile on his face fades. He just stands there, but he opens his arms up and I don't even think. I run into them. I close my eyes the instant he closes his arms around me, cradling me.

"It's going to be okay, Ellie."

"She knew that you called and didn't tell me. I thought she was someone who would always tell me everything."

"It doesn't matter anymore," he says, but I instantly shake my head no.

"It does. If I had known you called…"

"We can't go back, Ice. We have to look forward. We're different people now. At least, I know I am. I know what life is like without you now. You have to know I'll fight like hell to keep you in my life from here on out. I don't want to be without you again."

I tilt my head back to look at Liam. I want to see his face, I *need* to.

"We let the past die," I respond.

"We learn from it and we let it go," he corrects me.

"What comes next?" I ask, my heart beating harder all at once.

"You know the answer to that one, Ice."

"You want me to come back to Tennessee."

"Definitely. You liked it there. It was home, remember?"

"What if the club doesn't want me back?" I whisper, my biggest fear.

"Are you fucking kidding me right now, Ice? The boys love you."

"So much has happened, changed…" I'm trying not to panic at the thought of going back to Tennessee, but I definitely am.

"You'll like the changes. You'll love Rory and you'll definitely love Torrent. Not being wanted is the *very* last thing you need to be worried about," he says, doing his best to dismiss all of my worries.

"But—"

"I mean it, Ice. It's all going to be okay."

I sigh, because he's not going to let me argue with him and right now, I really don't want to either.

"What *should* be my biggest worry about going back home, Liam?" I mumble derisively. I'm grudgingly letting it all go for now.

"If you're going to able to walk by the time I get tired of fucking you."

"You're going to get tired of fucking me?" I ask immediately, making him laugh. I end up squealing as he picks me up and deposits me on the kitchen table, yanking his shirt I'm wearing over my head.

"Maybe, after a couple of lifetimes," he mutters, taking my mouth in a kiss. I lose myself in his touch and the pleasure only he has ever been able to give me. I have to believe that everything will work out.

I don't have a choice.

FURY

"*W*hat are you doing, Brother?" Devil asks. I grip my phone with one hand and shake my dick, then zip up with the other.

"What the hell do you think I'm doing?" I grumble.

"Standing outside with your dick in your hand, taking a piss?"

"Very funny, motherfucker. I tell you what I'm not doing, I'm not in bed making Ellie suck me off as a thank you for the way I wore her out last night."

"Yeah, I know, that's because you're standing there taking a piss."

I jerk around when I realize that Devil is coming around the side of the building.

"Jesus," I growl, hanging up the phone.

"Diesel would have your ass if he knew how easy we snuck up on you, dude," Rebel laughs.

"Fuck you both." I laugh, walking toward them. "What in the hell are you doing here?"

"We came to check up on you," Devil says.

"I'd shake your hand but...."

"Leave me out of it. I don't want near anywhere your dick has been," Rebel laughs. "I know you and Scorpion don't mind getting close when it comes to that shit, but that's not for me."

I flip Rebel off, ignoring the guilt I feel with his words. I didn't truly lie to Ellie, but I might have left out a few details. I need to talk to this motherfucker before he says something that will screw up my future. I make a note to do that, but for now, I need to make sure Devil is okay.

"Bullshitting aside, how are you and how in the hell did you convince Torrent to let you come out here? Last I heard you were going to Chicago."

"Gunner located Torrent's sister. He's got that under control from the sound of it. You spotted Wolf here..." He shrugs. "Figured this is where I needed to be."

"You need to be home taking care of your woman and LD."

"The name is Cannon."

"I'll start calling him that the day you convince Torrent to call him that, too," I compromise.

"Asshole," Devil laughs.

"Still no word from Wolf?" he asks, joking aside. There's a hardness that comes over him now. He's all business, and I see the old demons he carries enter into his face. I hate that he has the memories he has, I fucking hate that he had to live through that shit and I couldn't get to him sooner. I want to kill that motherfucking Wolf for that reason alone.

"Not a one. Not since he questioned one of the nuns."

"It's not really his M.O. Fuck man, I don't know. Maybe he spotted me and got spooked?"

"If he saw you, he's plotting for a way to get to you. He won't run until he thinks he's close to getting trapped. This motherfucker is as arrogant as they come. He likes dancing along the edge," Devil replies, sounding completely confident. "Wolf will wait around to find a weakness and then the bastard will find the best way to exploit it.

"That means I need to keep a closer eye on Ellie then, because that's the only weakness I have."

"It might not be a bad idea," Devil says, rubbing the back of his neck. "I still can't believe you and Ellie are back together," he says and this time he's studying me. I can't help the satisfied smile that spreads over my lips.

"He looks fucking satisfied about it, too," Rebel says with a laugh.

"You have no idea," I respond, not even bothering to deny it.

"I'm happy for you, man. I know how losing Ellie cut you up."

"It nearly destroyed me. I'm not letting her go again." We stare at each other for a minute, not talking, but we understand each other. I know he can see in my face more than I feel comfortable telling him in words. Devil knows how much losing Ellie shook me. "How long have you been here?"

"Just got in. Came to the church first, because I knew that's where you'd be."

"Then let's go get you—" I stop when my phone rings. When I see Ellie's name on the ID, I answer it, holding up my finger toward my brothers. "Give me just a second. What's up, Ice?"

"Just checking on you, Stud. Was afraid you'd fall asleep after the way I left you worn out yesterday."

"Think you got that backwards, baby," I murmur, my head dropping down with a smile as I replay making love to her this morning in my mind.

"I just wanted to tell you that I love you, Liam."

"Love you, too, Ice."

"I love you, too, Eleanor!" Devil calls out.

"Oh my God! Is that Devil?" Ellie squeals in my ear.

"Yeah, baby. That's Devil. He and Rebel just showed up. I was about to take them and get them settled in a hotel and then maybe finding lunch—"

"No way! If you do that, Charles Liam Maverick, I'll never talk to you again. I've got three spare bedrooms. Take them to the house."

"Ice—"

"Don't you Ice me."

"Okay, Ellie, but if you start bitching, saying I can't fuck you because they might hear, you and I are going to have problems," I growl. The guys instantly start laughing, but I ignore them.

"You'll just have to get inventive on ways to keep me from crying out," she sasses.

"Oh, I can do that."

"Don't be so sure," she cautions.

"You can't scream when you're choking on my cock," I tell her.

"I can't believe you just said that in front of them."

"If that embarrasses you—"

"I didn't say I was embarrassed, just that I can't believe you. I got to get off of here, Harvey is giving me mean looks. Take the boys to the house, got it?"

"Got it, Ice."

"Love you, Liam."

"Love you, too," I tell her, hanging up and doing it while smiling.

"Fuck," Devil hisses.

"You can say that again," Rebel adds.

"What?" I ask.

"It's just really good to see that look on your face again, man," Devil replies.

"What look?"

"The look that says you're a man who has his balls locked up tight in his woman's purse but that you don't give a fuck."

"You got all that from the smile on my face?"

"I see it every day in the mirror," he says with a shrug.

"Well, you two keep away from me. I like having my balls right where they are," Rebel jokes, but Devil and I share a smile because we know exactly what Rebel is missing. All I can feel is pity for the asshole.

WOLF

I forgot how satisfying it is to spend the night fucking a warm cunt over and over until my balls cry out in protest. It helps when the cunt in question likes it dirty. I lean back against the headboard. The sexy redhead is on her stomach, a pillow pushed under her so my cum running out of her pussy is gathered there. I'm not about to sleep on the fucking wet spot. I did fill her full though. Partly because I could. I'd not had a good fuck in months, but I have to admit I did it mostly because it was fun to watch her bitchy girlfriend eat her pussy out and have to swallow down my jizz.

Dawn.

Raven hair, bitchy mouth, but big tits. She hates me. It's clear to see all over her face. She despises me. She is only agreeing to this party because it's what the redhead wants. What was her name? Glenna. Yeah, that's it. She's a good fuck, but she's not the one I'm having fun with. That would be Dawn. It's a pity that she hates me. Her and I are so much alike. Fuck, we could be soulmates. I see the darkness in her, I can fucking smell it. It makes my cock hard and that's the real reason I was able to fuck the red head over and over. Each time I filled her pussy full of my cum, it twisted the knife inside of Dawn a little more. It fueled the anger inside of her and whether she realizes it or not…it's drawing her closer to me.

I'm going to turn her into the perfect pet before the day is over.

The mere thought of that makes my poor, abused, slut-soaked cock instantly hard. I reach down and stroke it, stretching out the kinks and getting ready for round…hell, I don't even know what number.

"Jesus, doesn't that thing ever die?" Dawn snarls, coming back into the room. She got up early this morning to shower and gargle. I offered to join her and she threw her phone at me.

"Why don't you hop on and I'll take you for a ride? I've worn out your girlfriend's cunt. You haven't let me near yours."

"Nothing gets inside of me that might kill me."

I bark out a laugh, because really this bitch has no idea. *But she might learn.*

She begged her girl to use condoms last night. When I threatened to walk, the redhead immediately caved. Dawn wouldn't come near my cock, but I doubt she would have even if I had gloved up. She sure as hell didn't turn down eating out the cumsoaked pussy. She hated it, but she was desperate to remind her girlfriend that she was still in the room.

It had to be a blow to Dawn's ego to realize the woman she loved couldn't have given a fuck if she was here or not.

"Don't tell me you're that scared of dicks. I won't believe that shit. Your girl told me you used to have a man, before her sweet little snatch lured you to the dark side."

"Please, you're making me sick," Dawn mutters, flopping down on the bed beside me, although not too close. The redhead lets out a loud snore and I watch as Dawn narrows her eyes at her. She's so fucking pissed, she could choke the woman herself. I see it.

Suddenly, I'm in an even bigger mood to play. I let my hand wrap in the pretty auburn strands of the sleeping girl, then I pull.

"Ow," the bitch cries. She slowly focuses on me, smiling and practically purring, as her dilated eyes open wider.

"How's my pretty playmate this morning?"

"Hungry," she moans.

"What do you want, Pet?" I ask her, yanking her hair tighter pulling back so she can see Dawn. "You want to eat your girl's pretty pussy?"

Oh if looks could kill, I wouldn't be breathing right now.

Dawn makes pushing her buttons so much fun.

"Glenna," Dawn says, but she's interrupted.

"No," Glenna whines, pulling on my hold to look up at me while licking her tongue.

"Does the pretty girl want more of my cock?"

Her body trembles like a fucking bitch pup in heat. When I glance over at Dawn, I decide it's time to make this a little more interesting.

I reach under the mattress. I put a couple of things I knew I would need there. It seemed the best place to hide them. I find the small vile of coke—laced with a little surprise. I grab the cap between my teeth and open it. Glenna's eyes are on me, but it's Dawn who is watching me so close the heat from her glare makes pre-cum leak down my cock.

"What the fuck is that?"

"Like you don't know," I laugh. "I think it's time to make this party even more fun."

"Fuck no. I didn't agree to that shit."

"You can't convince me you don't party. I know better."

"I didn't say that, but I didn't sign on for that this weekend," Dawn growls.

"You need to unwind. This will help and think about how much fun Glenna will be once the edge is taken off. She'll let you do whatever you want to her," I bait her.

"She'll let me do what I want, anyway. She loves me" Dawn

says, and it's fucking hard not to laugh out loud. I've done my research. I always do.

I use the firm hold I have on Glenna's hair to flip her over on her back. The hungry little slut is so ready she instantly spreads her legs, bending them at the knees and opening wide for me. I know Dawn doesn't miss that at all.

It makes her angrier.

"Strip, Dawn. Let me show you how much fun I can make things for you."

"I don't want your cock," she mutters, her eyes still glued to her girlfriend's pussy.

I put a line of coke on one of Glenna's pretty little tits.

"I can't reach it," she whines, pulling on my hold.

"Stop fighting me, bitch. You can have yours off the lips of Dawn's pussy. What do you say, Dawn?" I question her, my tone mocking.

"I need to check in with my sister," she says, her eyes never leaving the coke. Yeah, she's partied before and now she's definitely interested. It never ceases to amaze me how good I am at understanding what drives people.

"Do a line. While you're waiting for the hit to deepen, we'll send her a selfie of the three of us showing her you're both happy. Then, once that's out of the way, we'll let our little red-headed whore eat your neglected little pussy."

"What you will be doing?" she says, as if she's not convinced. We both know she is, but I push her even more. I know what she wants, even if I'm not sure she does. I'll be glad to show her, however.

"Drilling her ass without lube to punish her for ignoring you."

"You're a sadistic fuck," Dawn says, but I notice she's not telling me that I can't do it.

"You say that like it's a bad thing. Don't worry. I'll make her bleed for you. You'll like that won't you?" I ask her and I don't miss the light that sparkles in her eyes in that moment. What do you say, Dawn?"

"You sure this is what you want, Glenna?"

"Quit fucking around, Dawn. I want to party. You don't like it, get the fuck out," Glenna says, her words slurred from the hit of coke I gave her earlier. Dawn didn't know about that. She wasn't ready, but oh, she is now.

"Fine, whatever. You better make it good," Dawn growls and I reach over to the nightstand and give her the small cut-off straw. She takes it begrudgingly and snorts her line.

"Now get undressed."

"We have to take a picture for my sister," she reminds me.

"We'll get under the sheet."

"I want my coke, damn it," Glenna moans.

"You better hurry, or I'm going to fuck her without letting you play," I taunt Dawn. "And I doubt she'll notice you're even here after that."

"I hate you," Dawn growls, taking her robe off, throwing it on the floor.

"Where's your phone?" I ask her.

"Fuck that shit is powerful," Dawn says, already starting to float into the land of happy. I'll need to move fast if I'm truly going to enjoy this.

"Where's your phone?" I ask again.

"Night...nightstand drawer," she says, her head going back as she lets the hit settle.

I reach over and get it, then settle on the bed with Glenna between me and Dawn. I hold out the phone, aiming it so all three of us are reflected on the screen.

"Say cheese," I tell them and the bitches say it like my puppets, but then that's exactly what they are. I quickly send the photo to Ellie, satisfaction flooding through me. "There that's done. Let's get this party started!"

I lean down spreading some coke on the bare lips of Dawn's

pussy. She's wet, I can smell her. I think I'm going to fuck that cunt later, just for shits and giggles. I find the straw that Dawn left earlier and hand it to Glenna.

"Now?" Glenna pants.

"Definitely, now," I tell her, with a wink at Dawn.

This is going to be fun....

ELLIE

"You look way too happy, Ellie. I'm not used to that," Harvey says when I hang up.

"Gee thanks, Harvey," I mutter, getting a customer a shot of tequila.

"I mean it, what's going on? Hell, Trina says you haven't even complained of a migraine all week."

I hold my head down as I think about that. He's right. I've not really had a bad headache since I let Liam back in.

"I'm...." I stop for a minute as the gravity of what I'm saying hits me so strong that my knees threaten to buckle.

"Ellie?"

"I'm getting back together with my ex-husband."

"Shit. I didn't even know you had a man," Harvey mumbles, looking at me strangely.

"Yeah. He lives in Tennessee."

"Hold up. Is he dragging his ass up here?"

"I...We haven't talked a lot about it yet, Harvey, but if things work out..."

"You're going to leave me," Harvey mutters.

"Yeah, I...I'll go back to Tennessee."

"Is he good to you, Ellie?"

"Really good," I tell him, without so much as a pause.

"You're going to have to introduce me to him, Ellie. I'm okay with losing you if he's a good man, but I'm not letting some asshole get his hands on you and hurt you all over again."

"Careful, Harvey. You almost sound like you have a heart there," I tell him with a grin.

"You're a good woman, even if your family is a little out there. At least they're all hot to look at. How is that mom of yours? Still single?"

"Ew. Don't even think about it."

"What? You don't think I'm good enough for her?" he demands, and I can't tell if he's upset or if he's yanking my chain.

"You know better, but I know too much about you."

"Like what?" he asks, but I can see the smile he's trying to hide.

"Like the fact that you like sex a lot."

"You say that like it's a bad thing, Ellie," he says, laughing so hard that his belly shakes. Harvey is a big man, almost as tall as Liam. He's also heavy and I don't know a man around who wouldn't worry about taking him on. He looks like a defensive lineman for the Dallas Cowboys—only his gear and padding are all real.

"It's not unless the woman in your bed is my mother. Then, it's just gross."

"Everyone needs love, even moms."

"I just don't want to know about it. With you I would and I've worked here long enough to hear about your kinky side, too, Harvey. You and my mom? That would scar my soul."

"Fuck you," he laughs. "Get to work. For now, you still work here and I'm not paying you to sit around and destroy my sex life."

"Yeah, right," I laugh, feeling my phone vibrate in my back pocket. I frown, because I just got off the phone with Liam. I take it out and see a message notification from my sister and relax. She's checking in. I mean I told her to, but I didn't think she actually would. My sister usually ignores me—especially when I'm pissed, and she knows I am pissed about her and Mom hiding the fact Liam called me.

I open the message and she didn't say anything, just sent me a picture. Proof she's pouting at me. We'll make up, of course, but I am hurt and it's going to take me a bit to get past it. Which probably makes me a bitch, considering my history with Liam...but, I can't help it.

I look at the picture and roll my eyes. Gross, they're all in bed together. I start to shut off the phone, when something catches my eye. It's the man that they're with. I know that guy. Dawn gave me his name, it's the one that Liam did the check on. *Reggie.* I know he came back cleared, but...

The guy in this picture is the same one that showed up at the club. He introduced himself to me. He's the same creepy guy that set off every internal alarm bell I had and when he told me his name, he didn't mention the name Reggie.

He said Charlie.

Maybe it's nothing. Maybe I'm overreacting. But the longer I stare at this picture, the more I can feel the panic build up. Why would he lie about his name? I mean, maybe he's like Liam and Charlie is a first name and Reggie his middle. But, if he goes by Reggie....

I text her, thinking if she texts back I'll relax, that it's all just a big misunderstanding.

Are you okay, Dawn?

It feels like forever while I wait for a return message. When nothing comes, I look to make sure I have signal. I miraculously have a full bar lit up.

But still no reply.

Then, I take in the fact that in the picture they're all smiling but the guy—whoever, he is—his smile is different. It's harsher, darker, and he looks...

Evil.

"Ellie, what's wrong?" Harvey asks. I stare at my sister's picture, use my fingers to enlarge it. Something isn't right with her. She looks out of it. My heart squeezes in my chest.

"Harvey, I have to go. Something is wrong with Dawn," I tell him. I move from the bar, never looking up at Harvey. I stop moving at all when a text comes back. My heart is pounding, blood thundering in my ears, almost drowning out the notification, as I check the message.

Dawn's a little busy. See you soon, Eleanor.

My hand is so tight on my phone it's painful. My entire body is trembling.

Did I tell this guy my full name?

The whole conversation is a blank right now.

I want to talk to Dawn.

He doesn't reply. The message shows delivered, but not read.

Fuck this.

I dial the phone. It goes straight to voicemail. With shaking hands, I try again.

Same thing.

There's a slim chance they're all having sex and I'm being the moron sister who likes to control shit too much, but I know in my heart something is wrong. I could call Liam, but I don't know how to explain it. He might think I'm getting upset over nothing. I just know that I'm not. Something is wrong.

I know it.

I make it to my car, with Harvey yelling after me. It's only then that I realize I'd been running. Still, Harvey is about to catch up with me, but I am in my car and peeling out of the parking lot before he has a chance to stop me.

Please, God, let my sister be okay. Let me be wrong.

WOLF

$\mathcal{I}$ shut off Dawn's phone, wishing I could see Eleanor's face at the moment. It's sad that I can't. She's smart enough to know this is going to go bad. She's probably running to her little fuck-buddy now. I've stayed ahead of the Savage Brothers for over a year now. They're so useless. If she thinks they are going to be able to help her now, she's in for a big surprise.

The two bitches I'm with are moaning on the bed. For Glenna, I'm thinking it's all about the drugs coursing through her system, she's had far more than Dawn. For Dawn? She's finally got her woman back. I'll have fun taking that from her in a bit, but for now let her have her fun. I carry Dawn's phone over to the cheap dresser and using the pocket knife I put there earlier, I pry open the back panel of her phone and take the battery out.

I can't have them trying to trace the fucking thing and ruining the party too soon. I already threw Glenna's away before we even began our fun.

I walk back over to the bed and I can tell Dawn is close to coming. Glenna has her head buried between Dawn's legs, and Dawn has her fingers wrapped in her lover's hair. She looks so happy, pleasure and drugs thrumming through her. It's time to introduce her to a little bit of pain.

"I'm starting to feel left out girls," I announce, smiling when Dawn opens her eyes to glare at me.

Glenna looks up from Dawn's pussy, letting out this overly-loud annoying giggle.

"We can't have that. Lay down and I'll climb on board," she tries to purr. Her words are slurred, even though I weakened her last dose. If I gave her just a little more, it might kill her. There wouldn't be much fun in that. What I have planned for this little redhead is much better.

But then, you'd have to give up eating Dawn out and she was enjoying that. Aren't you, Dawn?"

"Come back down here, Glenna," Dawn says, she's trying her best to sound pouty, but I hear the thread of anger that she can't disguise no matter how high she is.

"I want Reggie to fuck me. C'mon, Reggie. Dawn will get even more excited watching you fuck me," she whines.

I don't think Glenna's that clueless, she just doesn't give a damn. That's causing Dawn's hate to come through loud and clear. It's not all directed at me now, however. That fact plays right into my plans.

"That wouldn't be fair." I smack her on the ass so hard that the palm of my hand burns. "Get up on your hands and knees," I order her and she eagerly does what I ask. I position myself behind her, while I slide my hand against her pussy. Even though she's wet, she's nowhere near what she was when I was fucking her last night.

"That feels good," she purrs.

"You're not very wet," I respond with a smirk, my gaze boring into Dawn's. I figured eating Dawn out would have you all prepped for me."

"I wanted you," Glenna says and oh, that has to hurt. I can see Dawn wince with pain, even though she tries to hide it.

"You're such a dirty little slut, aren't you Glenna?"

"All for you, baby," she murmurs, her head going back in pleasure as I drag my fingers against her clit.

"I think it's time you're punished for neglecting Dawn."

"I didn't neglect her," she cries. "I ate her out just like you told me to!"

"But, you didn't make her come. Now, you don't get dick until she's happy."

Dawn's watching me with a funny look on her face. She doesn't trust me and she really shouldn't. I'm about to make her get in touch with who she really is and that is going to be painful for her. Fortunately, it's going to be a fuck of a lot of fun for me.

"That's not right."

"Do as I tell you," I order.

Dawn is sitting on the bed now instead of lying. But when Glenna sees that she's not going to get what she wants, she turns back to Dawn. "Fine, I'll do it," she huffs. "This is your fault," she mumbles, giving Dawn a pissed look.

"Forget this, I'm done," Dawn growls, finally getting tired, all of her pain at this point is replaced with anger. I can't let her leave, though. I have plans and she's not going to ruin it.

By this time, I've moved behind Dawn. I put my hands on each of her shoulders, lean down and whisper in her ear. "If you're going to cut the bitch out of your life, at least have some fun with it. Let's make her pay for not showing you the respect you deserve," I purr, tempting her with the one thing I know she can understand.

Revenge.

"What would you know about it?" she asks, sparing me a look. Glenna is working between Dawn's legs, clueless to the fact that Dawn isn't into it any longer.

"Let's just say, I know what it's like not to be respected and when that happens, you have to make others pay. You can't let people walk on you in this world, Dawn. If you do that, you're weak. I don't think you're weak, are you?"

"Fuck, no," she growls.

"Then, turn around and let's make the little bitch pay for disrespecting you."

"What's your plan?"

"We get her to admit all the wrongs she's done to you and then, we punish her."

"What does that even mean?" Dawn asks and I couldn't stop myself from laughing if my life depended on it.

"You don't worry your pretty little head over it. You just lie back against me and enjoy yourself. I'll take you exactly where you are meant to be."

She finally does as I tell her, though she's not quite relaxed as I want her to be. I can't have her fighting me. I don't have time for that. I need to be gone by the time Fury shows up. These idiots are slow, but there's no point in tempting fate.

I find the forgotten vile of coke from earlier and tap some out on my finger. When I turn my attention back to Dawn, Glenna is going to work between her legs and she's starting to unwind. Her eyes are closed, but they open immediately when I wrap one arm around her front, pressing my semi-hard cock against her back, and rubbing my fingers across her nipple.

"What are you—"

Her body shudders as Glenna thrusts her fingers inside of her. I squeeze her tit in a bruising hold.

"You need to unwind," I tell her. "You need to be loose to enjoy this next part." I take the coke that's on the tip of my finger and hold it in front of her nose.

"Am I doing good, Reggie? Do I get more?" Glenna asks.

"Dawn says when you can have more," I tell her, letting Dawn think she holds all the power. "C'mon, Dawn, just a little hit. You only live once," I murmur, teasing her nipple.

"I really fucking hate you," she growls, but she takes the hit.

I wait, biding my time until the drugs combine with what's already in her system. I can tell the minute the rush hits her. She relaxes completely in my arms. I move under her, settling her on my lap. I use my hands to pet her body as she grips her fingers in Glenna's hair. I slide my cock inside her cunt. She's so far gone, I wonder if she realizes at all what's going on, but then she squeezes her cunt against my cock and I know the truth. She may prefer pussy, but the bitch likes to ride a hard cock too.

"Why does she get the coke and your dick?" Glenna huffs. "That's bullshit. She's getting what belongs to me. You wouldn't even be here, if it wasn't for me."

"I like her pussy. It's much tighter," I growl into Dawn's ear, biting down on the lobe hard enough to draw blood. She shudders over me, adjusts so she's sitting up, taking control of riding me. I run my fingers down her back, looking over her shoulder at the anger boiling in Glenna's eyes. There's one thing you can always count on with a redhead, their temper can be legendary.

Right now, I'm banking on that.

"It's only tighter because she hates dick, she'd rather be smothered in pussy. She's terrified of cocks."

"She doesn't seem terrified now. She's riding me like a fucking rodeo star. You want my cock, Glenna, and another hit of coke?"

"Yes. I've earned it. I did what you asked."

Dawn slows down as she tries to understand what we're saying. She's definitely high as a fucking kite though. Which is good. *Really good.* Time to step things up.

"You crave dick so much, Glenna, how in the hell did you end up in a relationship with another girl?"

"I needed Dawn," she mutters.

"Why?"

"I care about her," she says, but she's lying. We both know it.

I hold up the empty vile. Of course, Glenna has no idea the vile is empty.

"You want this?"

"Yes," she says, her voice almost begging. She reaches for it and I hold it just out of her reach.

"Then, tell the truth. Tell Dawn why you're with her. She deserves to hear the real reason." Dawn's not riding me half as much now, but it doesn't matter, I'm getting more pleasure out of what's going on right now than I'd ever find in her cunt. This is just starting to get fun.

"I was kicked out of my apartment. I needed a place to stay, she'd been sniffing around me for a fucking month. I'd never tried being with a girl before, so I did."

"And you liked it?" I prod her, moving fingers over Dawn's pussy, keeping her primed.

"No," Glenna sighs. Dawn's body goes tight in my arms but I hold her down on me. She's not getting away.

"Then, why in the fuck did you move in with me?" Dawn snarls.

"I needed you to co-sign to buy my car. You were so fucking easy. All I'd have to do is pretend to enjoy getting you off and you'd give me anything."

"You used me," Dawn whispers, the sadness bleeding through the happiness the drugs had going just moments before.

"Can I have the coke now?" Glenna says, dismissing Dawn.

"You hate Dawn, don't you?" I purr, grabbing her hair and pulling her so that her face is right in front of me, but even closer to Dawn.

"Yes. I hate everything about the bitch. I thought getting a man in our bed would make her leave, but she's so weak, she stayed even knowing she wasn't wanted," Glenna snarls.

"You fucking bitch," Dawn cries out. Then, surprising even me, she wraps her hands on each side of Glenna's neck and starts choking her.

Glenna flails, clawing at Dawn's hands, but Dawn doesn't let go. Glenna's face is starting to change color, she's gasping and making these noises that I swear to fuck, vibrate in my cock.

"She used you," I purr in Dawn's ear. "She thinks you're weak."

"I'm not weak!" Dawn screams, and even from this angle I can see the tears sliding down her face. "I'm not weak!"

"You need to teach this bitch a lesson. She's a user. I bet she's even been fucking men while you're been together. While you're out working to pay off her car, she's home fucking whatever cock she can find."

"I'll kill you," Dawn hisses to Glenna and she's really close to doing just that if the color of Glenna's skin is to be believed.

"You need to make it hurt," I whisper, ever helpful. I reach under the mattress and find the knife I have hidden there.

"She's not worth it," Dawn finally says, and drops her hands, one falling on my leg.

"I knew you couldn't do it," Glenna says, her voice hoarse. She coughs as she gets the words out. "You're too fucking weak. That's why I picked you. I could control you," she hisses. I put the knife in Dawn's hand, wrapping her fingers over the handle. She jerks, looking down at the knife in her hand. I put my other hand back in Glenna's hair, keeping her from moving away. The poor bitch hasn't seen the knife yet.

Soon she will.

"I hate you. I hated everything about you. The way you snore at night, the way you insisted on spooning me every night like a fucking loser. I hated it all, but the thing I hated the most was the way you tasted. I had to hide the fact that I was gagging the entire time!" Glenna is trying to scream, but her vocal cords are definitely bruised.

Dawn raises the knife, and presses it against Glenna's neck.

"I'm not weak now, am I, bitch? Do I look weak to you?" she snarls. She presses the blade deeper, and a little sliver of blood appears bright against the silver blade.

"Like you have the balls to do anything. You'll wimp out, just like you do with everything else," Glenna laughs.

I see the moment indecision flashes through Dawn. I may not

be able to see her face, but I feel it coming off of her in waves. I cap my hand over hers and hold the knife, not letting her retreat. I press harder. Glenna's worried now, I see it in her dilated eyes. She tries to pull away from me, but she's afraid to do too much because the knife is poised, cutting into her.

"It's time to take back control, Dawn. If you don't have respect in this world, you have to take it," I tell her. I move the knife down just a little, cutting Glenna as I go. I stop to see what she's going to do. I'm not going to let her out of this, but I'd like it better if she does this part of her own free will. It will make it that much sweeter.

"Dawn, baby, I did...n't mean it. Let's stop this...Go home."

"You mean the house I paid for? The bed I paid for, because you had to have it?" Dawn asks. "How many people did you fuck in our bed, Glenna? How many?" she cries.

"Dawn," Glenna whispers. She doesn't say anything else, but she doesn't have to. The truth is easy to read and I smile in victory.

"Who? Who did you take to our bed?" she asks. Glenna doesn't answer, but it's clear, even if high on coke, to see that there's been someone. Unless I miss my guess there were several. "I hate you," Dawn mumbles. "I fucking hate you."

"Not as much as I hate you," Glenna says, deciding finally that Dawn isn't going to buy more of her lies. She probably feels she's safer, too, because with my hand dropped off the blade, Dawn has lessened the pressure on Glenna's neck.

But the bitch should have kept her mouth shut. That's exactly what it takes to push Dawn over the edge. She slits Glenna's throat, in one hurried, but fluid movement. There's blood flowing down Glenna's pale white skin and with each drop my dick swells and distends inside of Dawn.

I knew this was going to be fun.

ELLIE

I don't remember the drive home. It's a blur. As I get out of the vehicle, all I know is that it feels like I can't breathe. There's a strange vehicle in the driveway with Texas plates, and I get scared that something is wrong here, and then mostly piece together that it's probably Devil's rental. I sprint to the front door and fumble with my key to try and open the door. In the end, it's yanked open and I almost fall because I was leaning on it to hold me up. My knees are too damn weak.

"Ice? What the fuck is going on?" Liam growls, taking my trembling body into his arms. His body heat surrounds me, but I still feel so cold that I wonder if I will ever be warm again.

"Liam," I cry, wrapping my arms around him.

He picks me up, cradling me against his body and carries me to the couch. He puts me down and then kneels down in front of me on his knees. It's only then that I realize that I'm crying. Which is crazy. I truly might be overreacting.

But it doesn't feel like I am.

"Baby, tell me what's going on? Harvey called and said you tore out of the parking lot like wild animals were chasing you."

"I think Dawn is in trouble, Liam. I think this Reggie or whatever is bad. I'm afraid he's really bad."

"Ice, we've talked about this. We checked him out and Dawn is going to do what she wants. She's not going to listen to you. In fact, knowing her, if you tell her not to do something, she'll do it anyway," Liam says. "I don't want you worrying and getting yourself all worked up and sick over this. Dawn is who she is. She's never going to change, you know that. She's always been her own worst enemy."

I hold my head down, trying to sort through my most chaotic thoughts and calm my mind, so I can make him understand. It's not easy, because right now breathing is hard. I almost feel as if I've run a marathon.

"Here ya' go, Ellie. Take a drink of this, beautiful."

I look up to see one of Liam's brothers. The face of the man that I've truly missed. From the first day that Liam and I got together, Devil became like a big brother to me and it hurt not hearing his smartass remarks day in and day out. At first I'm shocked by his appearance. He's changed so much, but not in a good way. His face has scars that are faded, so they've been there a while. He's wearing an eyepatch and because Liam told me a little about the torture that Devil endured, I know it's not just for looks. He's lost weight, too, but he looks good despite all of that.

"Devil," I murmur, taking the drink.

"Is that water?" I hear Liam ask.

"Hell, no. Ellie looked like she needed some whiskey."

He's not wrong. I take a small drink and swallow it down, hoping it helps.

"Thanks," I tell him.

"It's damn good to see you again, Eleanor," Devil says and I smile despite the fear that I'm feeling.

"You too, Devil. Leave it to you to resort to making yourself look like Captain Jack Sparrow just to get in all the girls pants," I joke weakly, as he grins.

"I'm a reformed man, darlin'. Finally found the one," he says and I can see that it's real. I'm happy for him. Liam squeezes my hand, getting my attention and I look at him, while handing Devil my drink back.

"I think she's really in trouble, Liam. She texted me a picture of the three of them with Reggie. It's the first time I'd really seen a picture of him and I know him."

"You know him? You mean he's a regular at the bar?"

"No, although I did meet him there. Do you remember when I told you about that weird guy that came in the other day? How he gave me the creeps?"

"Charlie, right? Yeah, I remember."

"Right. Except if his name is Charlie, then why is he going by the name Reggie with my sister."

"You're sure it's the same guy?"

"I'm sure. What's more is he looks just as creepy. There's something about him that just screams danger."

"Ellie maybe you're just seeing things that aren't there because you're worried about Dawn," he suggests gently. "It is possible he has two first names."

"Hold up, if this is the guy you had Scorpion run the check on, Fury, then he doesn't. He just has that god-awful name Reginald. Remember?" Rebel asks.

"Still, that doesn't mean Ellie should be freaking out," Liam says. "Maybe he was cruising for a woman when he met Ellie and didn't want to give his real name," he adds, but I can hear the doubt in his voice now. The fact that he's starting to sound worried makes my panic slowly eek back in.

"Something is wrong, Liam, I know it. Here, look at this picture. He's bad, I'm sure of it. You can see it on his face."

I sound crazy, I know. But, I've always been really good at judging people. I trust my gut when it comes to trusting or not trusting someone and it's never led me wrong.

Except maybe when it comes to my mother lying to me about Liam.

I take my phone and find the photo that Dawn texted to me earlier. My hands are shaking and it takes me longer than it should. I hand the phone to Liam and he grabs it, relaxing backwards on his feet as he looks.

"Fuck," Liam hisses.

"You've got to be fucking kidding me," Rebel says, crouching down to look at the phone.

I blink as the boys toss about the f word, it's not really new, but there's something about their voices this time that makes me even more scared. Devil must hear it, too, because he hadn't been paying attention before. But he looks down over Liam's shoulder and his entire body goes solid. I can literally see all movement from him stop. It's almost as if he turns to stone.

I gasp as he reaches down and snatches the phone out of Liam's hand.

"Motherfucker," he roars, gripping my phone so tight that I half expect it to turn to dust.

"What? *What?*" I cry, terrified. I reach out and grab Liam's arms needing some type of contact with him.

"Ellie," Liam says. His tone doing nothing to make my fear go away. If anything it chills me to the bone.

"Liam, what's going on?" I ask, afraid of the answer, but needing to know.

"That's Wolf, the guy I've been hunting, in that picture."

I have to fight to keep from passing out, my nails biting into Liam's arm.

"*Oh, God.*"

I'd never seen a picture of Wolf. I'm sure Liam probably had one when talking to people at the church, but I didn't truly want involved. Now, I'm kicking my own ass. It feels as if I'm caught in a horrible time loop. My words feel as if they're torn from my soul. They bleed out and each syllable is painful.

"Let's load up and get to them. I want this motherfucker in my hands before the sun goes down," Devil growls, already walking to the door.

"But," I respond, and I don't know if I'm talking loud at all. My heart is pounding in my ears and it's drowning out all other sound. "I don't know where they're at. Dawn wouldn't tell me. They could be anywhere, Devil. They might not even be in the city and this photo was almost an hour ago. Dawn could be…"

"Ice—"

I cut back to look at Liam, seeing the worry on his face and I whisper the one thing I'm thinking. "Dawn could already be dead."

I collapse then, letting the tears fall as if a dam has broken. Sobs rack my body and Liam takes me in his arms.

FURY

"**I** can't believe this motherfucker is going to get away again," Devil shouts, kicking one of Ellie's dining table chairs and causing it to fall backwards. I would slap him and tell him to get control of his shit because he's scaring Ellie, but I figure of all of us, he has more right to lose it when it comes to Wolf.

I'm on the phone to Scorpion, waiting as they try to ping Dawn's phone. I'm still on the couch, holding Ellie, and doing my best to keep her from completely losing it. She's still crying, but nothing like she did when we first discovered that it was Wolf the girls were with. I promised her I'd find Dawn and get her back safely, but the truth is I could be lying out of my ass. Wolf has a reason for targeting Ellie and then Dawn. My brother warned me of it, and I ignored him more or less. I'm not ignoring him now. Wolf found a way to exploit my biggest weakness. I'm going to make sure this motherfucker dies. Devil may have to fight me for the right to end him.

"Sorry, Fury. The phone is a no go. I get a general vicinity from the tower it last pinged off, but that's it," Scorpion says.

i

"Fuck."

"The good news is he's still in the same city. The bad news is he can be anywhere downtown. I shudder to think how many hotels are in downtown Phoenix."

"That's not enough to go on. Damn it, Scorpion, I need something to track this sack of shit," I growl.

"What about credit cards?" Ellie suggests. "Dawn has a couple and they'd probably use hers. I don't think Glenna has a card. She was in bad shape financially. I remember her and Dawn fighting over the bills Dawn was having to pay."

"You hear what she said, Scorp?"

"Yeah, you're going to have to give me a bit. This could take some time unless she knows the credit card information," he replies.

"Do you have her credit card info, Ice?"

"No," she says, the tears threatening to intensify again. "I know she has a Visa...I don't know the other. Discover maybe? I don't know, Liam."

"I'll work with that and expand. Give me thirty," Scorpion mutters. I can hear keys on a keyboard being typed on furiously. I know he's trying, but I don't have time to wait.

"Make it ten and call me back on my cellphone, we're heading downtown," I growl.

"You expect miracles," Scorpion mutters.

I hang up and I don't even have to look to know all eyes are on me.

"Let's load up. We'll head downtown and start checking out hotels. Scorpion will call when he gets more information," I tell them, helping Ellie to her feet.

"Ellie, you need—"

"Don't even try it. I'm going with you. This is my sister," she says, and I smile because even terrified, my girl still has a backbone of steel. My brothers are already outside and I hear their rental start up. Ellie and I quickly follow, piling into the back of the SUV.

"We have to find this motherfucker," Devil growls as Rebel peels out of the drive, barely avoiding careening into Ellie's car.

"We will," I tell him.

I just hope it's not too late.

ELLIE

$\mathcal{I}$'ve never been more terrified in my life. The ride downtown is silent and full of tension and even though I'm not crying any longer, I'm still terrified.

"Do you know of hotels down here that Dawn would choose?" Rebel asks.

"No. She's not really the type to go to hotels," I murmur, flinching when Devil lets out an annoyed breath. I know he's disappointed and mad. I wish I could magically just know, but I don't.

"This is all my fault. I should have insisted that Dawn give me all the information. I asked, but she just told me to mind my own business. She let me ask you to run a check on him, and I figured once he got the all clear..."

"It's not your fault, Ice. It's mine. I should have demanded a picture or something," Liam says, his voice sounding bleak as we wait in traffic for a light change.

"I'm fucking tired of how this son of a bitch is always one step ahead of us," Devil growls, slamming his fist down so hard against the car door that I worry the window will fall down.

The loud sound of Liam's phone ringing makes me jump. We

all look at him as he raises his phone and answers it, leaving the call on speakerphone so we can all hear.

"Speak," he barks.

"No card activity under Dawn's name, Wolf's, or the Glenna girl."

"Fuck. Why did you waste time running Wolf's anyway? He's not stupid," Devil snarls.

"No stone unturned and all that shit," Scorpion replies.

"Big fucking lot of good that does us. I guess we're checking out more hotels," Rebel mutters, cutting into another lane.

We've already checked two hotels while waiting for Scorpion to call back. There's been no sign of my sister. I lay my head on Liam's chest, trying not to feel like it's hopeless and we're already too late.

I'm afraid we are though.

"Well it's a good thing I am thorough assholes, because on a hunch I ran one Reginald Cleary's info and two days ago at the Hotel Palomar downtown, ol' Reggie rented a suite."

"Why in the fuck didn't you just say that?" Liam demands, but before Scorpion can reply he hangs up.

"Take this exit," I yell at Rebel. "It will be the quickest route to the hotel and miss most of the traffic."

Rebel does as I ask and we are at the backside of the hotel in no time.

"There's valet parking in the front," I tell him. But he's already coming to a stop.

Everyone is jumping out and I'm with them. Liam looks back at me, but I shake my head no. There's no way that I'm being left behind. I can see he's torn, but he knows better than to ask me to do that.

We sprint to the front door and I somehow make it to the front desk first.

"Reginald Cleary's room?" I ask, my voice sounding weird and frantic even to my own ears.

"I'm sorry, ma'am. I can't give out that kind of information.

"You'll give it or we're going to have problems," Liam orders.

"I'm sorry, sir, I can't," the clerk says, obviously nervous.

Liam leans in and drops his voice down to a deadly level. "That motherfucker up there is a known felon. He's left a trail of corpses from here to the East Coast. He has my sister-in-law up there in that hotel room and if you don't tell me what room he's in, you better believe we're going to have problems."

"Please help us," I plead, desperate. I watch as the clerk carefully takes out a hotel card. She types on the screen and runs the card through some kind of machine. She slides it across the counter to me.

"Room 714," she whispers. I grab the card with shaking hands, tears in my eyes. Then, I call out my thank you as we run toward the elevator.

Once we get inside, Liam takes the card out of my hand and he holds my face, framing it in his large hands.

"Ice, I need you to keep a clear head. You stay behind me the entire time. You let my body cover you and you hold onto my belt loop. You don't move away from me. Got it?"

"Got it," I reply, nodding my head.

The elevator ride seems to take forever. When the doors slide open, Liam moves quickly, but quieter than before down the hall. He draws his gun and my eyes automatically go beside me to where Rebel is and he has a gun drawn, too. We make it to the door, and Liam looks at me. I immediately get behind him, hooking my finger into his belt loop. He puts the card in the door and the small light turns green and I hear the clicking of the lock. I watch him turn the knob. There's no screaming coming from the other side. There's no noise at all. I'm terrified of what we will see when that door opens.

We're already too late.

FURY

I shove the door open so hard it slams against the wall. I step in, casing the place, finger on my trigger and cover every corner of the room. I hear Ellie gasp. She's spotted her sister. She's lying on the bed, covered in blood, holding Glenna. Ellie goes to them, and I curse under my breath as I use my body to shield her, giving her my back as I stay on alert.

Rebel goes around us after securing the door and putting the safety lock on. He goes into the bathroom. And a second later he calls out, "Clear!"

He walks back into the room, pulling the curtains open, to make sure Wolf isn't lurking behind them.

"Fuck," I hiss, shoving my gun in the back of my pants. "He's gone."

"Where's Devil?" Rebel asks.

"I think he missed the elevator. He doesn't move as fast as we do. He'll be here," I mutter.

"She's dead," Dawn says, so quietly that I almost miss what she's saying.

"Fuck, this is a mess. He slit her fucking throat," Rebel growls.

I reach down and touch Glenna's neck, for a pulse. I know it's useless, her eyes are open and glassy. There's no way she's alive. I am surprised because the body is warm, however.

"Dawn," I snap. Dawn ignores me, continuing to just rock Glenna in her arms. "Dawn," I growl more sternly. "When did Wolf leave?"

Dawn's dazed eyes come to me for a second, but then she turns away.

"Dawn, honey, when did Reggie leave?" Ellie asks more softly, holding Dawn's face and forcing her to look at her.

"He left right before you got here," she says, surprising the fuck out of me. I figured she'd be too looney to answer. It's obvious she's in deep shock. She might also be completely wrong and Wolf left hours ago. I have to see if we can find any signs of him, however. Plus, I doubt Wolf can get the drop on Devil, since Devil is looking for him, but I don't like the fact he's not here, yet.

"Ice—"

"Go, I'm calling 911. You see if you can find this bastard," she says, seemingly in complete control now that she knows Dawn is alive. "Keep the fucking door locked and I mean the safety lock. Follow me and do it the minute I go out."

She does immediately as I ask, and I know it's not the place for it, but I tilt down and kiss her quickly on the lips.

"Be safe," she says and then Rebel and I are out the door and down the hall. We take the stairs, wanting to make sure the motherfucker isn't hiding in them. If we don't find any sign of him, I'm going to personally go door by door. I won't let him get away again. He's haunted my family for way too long.

DEVIL

I lean against the cement pillar, waiting. I can't tell you for the life of me what makes me so positive that Wolf is going to show up, but I just know it. Suddenly everything around me is clear and I know without a shadow of a doubt that my waiting is over. Finally, after all of this time, I will have my hands on Wolf.

I should end him quickly and be done with it, but I won't. I'm going to take my time with the motherfucker and enjoy every minute of it. When we were going into the hotel, I saw the car parked at the edge of the alley. It's a silver Corvette. I mean, Wolf likes luxury and he loves to be flashy, and this is one of the best hotels in a huge city. That Vette could belong to anyone, but the vanity plates on the front snagged my attention.

Reggie 1.

Now, I might be wrong. There's probably a million Reggie's in Phoenix. But, considering Wolf is supposed to be here and he's been pretending to be this Reggie, and added in the fact that Reggie's card paid for this pricey as fuck hotel...I'm going to say it's a good chance that Wolf is the one driving this car. I'm torn between wanting to go to the hotel room with Fury and Rebel and needing to stay down here. Wolf has proven to be a slippery motherfucker. I can't take the chance of letting him get away. I grabbed my weapon that I despise, but am dying to use on Wolf, out of the back of the SUV. Now, I'm waiting. The longer time goes by without Wolf showing up, the more I'm starting to think I misjudged the sorry fuck yet again.

Then, all at once, I catch sight of a man in a blue suit, coming out of the back entrance of the hotel. He's changed since I last met him. His hair shorter, a little grayer in his beard, and definitely wearing dressier clothes. He's still the same bastard that has haunted my dreams for way too long, however. I stay hidden behind the pillar, listening as his footsteps bring him closer to me. Each one seems to take forever, even though I know better. Anticipation runs through me.

There's been a lot that has happened to me since I faced losing everything and dying. I've gone through so much, but I've found my way out of the blackness, thanks to having my Angel and now our little boy. Through it all, there's been this anger that I keep hidden. A darkness that keeps me from letting go of my past. It colors everything, even the happiness I've had. But, you better believe when the fucker comes close enough and I swing my bat— one covered in barbed wire, that has nails sticking out of it—the same one that the bastard used on me—I let that darkness take over. As I connect with Wolf's gut, and he falls down on the ground, I feel a twisted joy rise up inside of me.

"Honey, I'm home," I growl out, drawing my bat back and slamming into his face. I hit him another three times, before Fury and Rebel come out of the building. In the distance I can hear sirens beginning to get closer.

"I guess that answers the question about where you've been," Fury says and I look up at him and smile and this smile that isn't weighed down in the darkness, because now, I finally have Wolf right where I want him.

"Quit standing there playing with your dick. Get over here and help me get this motherfucker in the trunk of that Vette over there."

"What are you going to do with him?" Rebel asks. I lean down and find the keys to the Vette in Wolf's pocket. Next, I stomp my foot into Wolf's balls. He's unconscious so he doesn't cry like the little bitch he is, but I still enjoy grinding his balls into useless sacks.

"Anything I fucking want," I tell him, spitting on Wolf, just before my brothers help me load him up.

ELLIE

"*D*awn, honey. You need to get dressed," I tell her, my heart hurting as I see Dawn. She's still holding Glenna. She won't let her go.

"She's dead, Ellie."

"I know, Dawn. But, listen. The cops are on their way. You don't want to be naked when they come."

"The cops?" she asks, her eyes going wide. I see the fear there and I rush to reassure her.

"They have to come, Sis. Glenna is dead. We need to report it and make sure they know who did this."

"No. Don't call the police, Ellie. We can't let them find her. We have to hide her."

"It's too late, Dawn. We have to let this play through. Glenna is gone. We have to report the man that did this. We have to make sure that he can't hurt any other women."

"I...Reggie. Reggie did this. They'll understand that," she says and I blink. It's then I see the white reside on her nose. *Dang it.* I look around the bed and don't see anything, but on the floor almost under the bed is an empty vile and an old straw.

"Dawn, are you high?" I ask.

"He made us. He said he would kill us and then.... Glenna's dead," she moans. "She's dead, Ellie."

"I know, Dawn. I'm so sorry."

"She dead. He killed her, Ellie. He killed her."

"Put this on, Dawn," I tell her softly, realizing that she's too messed up to make sense at this point. She finally pulls away from Glenna and I wrap the robe around her. "Sit down in that chair. I'm going to get a cloth to wash your face." She nods, her gaze never turning away from Glenna, but walking like a zombie to the chair.

I quickly go to the bathroom to wet a washcloth. When I walk back into the room, I stop abruptly. Dawn is standing at the bed, she's pulled the sleeve of her robe down—almost like a glove—and she's holding a knife. She's using the tail end of the robe to wipe it clean. She puts it down beside Glenna, and just keeps staring at it.

"Dawn. What are you doing?"

"I..." her face jerks up to look at me, panic written all over her. I'm starting to get an uneasy feeling in my stomach. I hate myself for what I'm imagining right now, but I can't help it.

Why would Dawn wipe the knife clean?

"I can't stand to see her blood," Dawn says and I nod, but my gaze moves down to the now bright red stain on the robe.

FURY

"*Y*ou're quiet, Ice."

Ellie flips over to her side, stretching one leg over my waist, her hand on my shoulder, her head burrowed against my neck.

"I'm sorry, Liam. I just..." She gives a heavy sigh, before struggling to find the words to finish. "My sister is a mess."

"Wolf is good at fucking with people's minds. She'll heal," I tell her, although I'm not completely sure. I do think she will get better, but I'm not sure how anyone gets over seeing someone they love murdered.

"Maybe..." Ellie says, dragging her finger through the hair on my chest. "The police aren't going to find Wolf, are they?"

"There won't be anything left of him for them to find," I tell her. "But, they will try. He's wanted for the murders of Reginald Cleary and Glenna. They'll investigate until they can't find any leads."

"They won't see the fight at the back of the hotel on surveillance cameras of the hotel or the surrounding buildings?"

"Nope," I tell her, not elaborating. There's no point. "Why are you so worried?"

"I don't want you to get in trouble. Any of you really. Wolf has already ruined enough of Devil's life. I don't want anything else to happen."

"Trust me, Ice. It's going to be okay."

"Do you think Dawn is telling the truth?"

"What do you mean?"

"I don't know. Something just seems off, Liam."

"She's been through some heavy shit, Ellie. You can't really judge her right now. I think she might still be in shock."

"Yeah, maybe."

"Is there something you want to tell me, Ellie?"

"I don't know anything, not really. It's just, I can't get it out of my head at the way Dawn was cleaning off the murder weapon. Is that normal?"

"Fuck if I know, Ellie. Dawn lived through a nightmare. I have no idea what normal would be after that."

"You're right. She's not talking to me, so maybe that's what has me all screwed up. She even asked me to leave her alone. I just don't know what to do."

"I know it sucks, Ice, but you can't do anything. You just leave her alone and let her work shit out. She'll either reach out to you or she won't."

"That answer sucks, Liam."

"I know, baby."

"So, what comes next?" She asks and I let out a sigh.

"I'm going to need to go back to Tennessee, Ellie."

"We knew this day was coming," she says, and the sadness in her voice hurts.

"You said you'd come back with me," I remind her.

"Liam, I can't just leave right now."

We shift on the bed so that I can look at her. I want to see her face and more importantly, I want her to be able to see mine. I need to try and reach her.

"Why, Ice? What can you do here?"

"Well, I mean, I know the police are focused on finding Wolf and my sister isn't really in trouble, but she goes this week for an interview with the lead detective. She will need an attorney. Her mental state is not good and that's being nice. There's just a lot of chaos. Plus, I need to give Harvey at least two weeks' notice, I can't just leave him high and dry. He's been good to me."

"If I stay here for another two weeks and help you get packed and ready to move, will you come home with me then?" I ask, but I think I already know the answer.

"I can't give you an answer on that right now, Liam. I need to make sure that Dawn is safe. I need to make sure she's okay before I just leave."

"Did you call your mom?"

"Yeah," she says with a heavy sigh.

"And how did that go?"

"Not great. She's coming down at the end of the week to be with Dawn for her meeting with the detectives. She refuses to talk to me about you calling."

"We can't change the past, Ellie," I warn her.

"I know. I just hate that they lied to me, Liam."

"It's more like they just kept secrets and hid things from you."

"Semantics and you know it. Not telling me something is just as bad as lying when it affects your life, Liam. Dawn and my mother did it knowing it would."

"I don't want to leave Arizona without you, Ellie," I tell her and I don't bother keeping the pain out of my voice.

"It's not a permanent separation, Liam. I'll come back to Tennessee, I will. It just may take me a bit."

"You don't come home soon, Ellie, and I swear to you, I'll come back and drag your ass back home."

"Liam," she says with a smile, leaning up to kiss me. "I promise I will come home to you. I have to. I love you."

"Promise me, Ellie."

"I promise, Liam," she says solemnly. I hate like hell that this is where we're at. I don't want to leave her side for a minute.

"How long?"

"What?" she says surprised.

"How long do you need, and if you say a year, so help me God, Ellie, I will wear that ass of yours out."

"Are you asking me to give you a timeline of when I'll be back to Tennessee?"

"Is that a problem?"

"Well, kind of. How am I supposed to know how long it will take to get my sister settled and everything done so I can move?"

"Two weeks. You can get all that done in two weeks and give your notice to Harvey," I tell her, wondering how in the fuck I'm supposed to survive two weeks without her.

"Liam, I don't want to be away from you, but I need longer than two weeks."

"So give me a time," I tell her, trying not to panic at being without her even longer.

"Two months?" she says, tentatively.

"Fuck, no. There's no way, Ice. I'm not living without you for two fucking months."

I watch as her eyes dilate and she swallows nervously.

"Okay, one month."

"That's a long time," I mutter.

"It's thirty days. That's not that long, Liam. We've been apart almost two years. Thirty days should be a walk in the park."

"If the park is in hell, maybe," I grumble, making her laugh.

"I'll call you every night and we can Facetime. It will go quickly, Liam. You'll see."

"Will you facetime, naked?"

"Uh…"

"You want to stay away from me for a whole month, Ellie. You better fucking give me this at least."

"You have to be alone in your bedroom if I do," she demands.

"Fuck woman, it's not like I'm going to let anyone see you naked but me."

"Fine, then I'll Facetime you naked."

"The month starts tomorrow. If I have to leave, then the countdown starts tomorrow, too."

"Do you have any more demands, Liam?" she jokes.

"Fuck yes, I do."

"You do?"

"Damn straight. You're going to keep your body away from me for a whole damn month, woman. You better get on your knees and worship your man's cock."

"You're so romantic, Liam," she giggles, moving over top of me, her blonde hair falling down around her face and against my chest. Our gazes lock, and I see the heat slowly building in her.

"You want romance, Ice?" I ask her, my voice suddenly going hoarse as I look into her beautiful eyes.

God I love this woman.

"Yes, but where you're concerned, Liam, I want it all," she murmurs against my skin as she starts kissing down my chest and sliding between my legs.

"If you want romance, Ellie, I'll give it to you."

"You will?" she asks, her voice teasing as her hand wraps around my cock and she strokes me, my head rubbing against her stomach.

I watch as she moves further down, holding my cock now, while she leans in to lick the head, running her tongue and gathering the pre-cum that's glossed over the head.

"I definitely will, Ellie," I tell her, my eyes closing as she sucks the head into her mouth.

"What kind of romance?" she asks, her tongue licking up the underside of my shaft.

"I'll wipe your mouth after you swallow down my cum," I tell her, but that last part might come out as a muffled cry, because she's taking my cock into her mouth and it feels like fucking heaven.

She hums against my shaft and takes me all the way to the back of her throat, sucking so hard that my body shudders from the pleasure.

"That's it, baby, suck that cock and make your man come," I croon, watching her.

The entire time, all I can think is that there's no way I'll be able to be without her for a solid fucking month.

ELLIE

I stare at the calendar with a sick feeling in my stomach. It's been three weeks and I'm nowhere close to ready to move to Tennessee. That's not going to make Liam happy. Honestly, it doesn't make me happy. There's just so much going on and I can't see any way around it all.

If I want to be brutally honest, there's a part of me putting off going back because I'm afraid. I can't explain that to Liam. He wouldn't understand and I can't explain it to him. If I did that…*He might hate me.*

I look at my bedside clock. It's almost midnight. Liam was supposed to call at eleven. He said he was doing some things for Devil tonight though, and might be late. Our last conversation was kind of stilted. Mostly because I haven't given him a concrete answer on what day I'll be heading that way. I hate that I'm putting him through this.

I hate that I'm putting myself through it.

As the minutes tick by, I get this sick feeling in my stomach. There's every chance in the world that he won't call tonight. I can't even blame him. I know I'm going to have to go back soon. I can't truly give Liam up and staying here out of fear isn't helping either of us. I don't want to lose him because I'm being a coward. I roll over on the bed and punch my pillow in frustration. I had forgotten how lonesome my bed was without Liam in it. There's a lot I'd forgotten... like how I feel half alive without him.

I bolt upright when the phone rings, reaching over to grab it immediately.

"Hi, sweetheart," I murmur immediately, feeling a wave of relief push through me."

"Hey, Ice." His voice is gruff and I know immediately that tonight's conversation is going to go a lot like last night's.

"I was afraid you weren't going to call."

"Would you have missed me if I didn't?" he asks. I let out a breath, as a wave of sadness hits me.

"Of course I would have, Liam. I miss you every day. I hate being away from you." I pray that he can hear the sincerity in my voice. I'm not so sure he's looking for it, though.

"If you say so."

"What's that supposed to mean?"

"It means that you say you don't like being away from me, but here we are apart and that's on you, Ellie."

"Why does it have to all be on me?" I ask, immediately defensive.

"Don't start that shit, Ellie. We had this settled before I left there."

"You mean that *you* had it settled."

"You can't twist this around, Ellie. You said you'd be here in a month. That month is fast approaching and you're nowhere near ready to come home."

"Liam, you have to understand—"

"I've been trying to understand, Ice. I really have. I'm tired of being alone."

"Don't you think I am, too?" I ask him, and I close my eyes because suddenly I just feel...defeated.

"I don't know what you are, Ellie. You're the one choosing to stay there. It doesn't matter what I say, you're just...Fuck, I don't know what you're doing."

"Liam, I want to be with you, I do. It's just. The police want to question Dawn again. Not to mention, the manager Harvey hired screwed shit up. I'm trying to fix up all of his alcohol orders, while interviewing new applicants. It's just not a good time to move right now."

"You said your sister won't even talk to you."

"Well, she's not. But, I don't want her to go there by herself. She needs someone to have her back."

"And why does that have to be your job again, Ellie?"

"Liam, she's my sister."

"I get family loyalty, babe. I have that in spades, but if you don't get that loyalty back, then you sure as fuck don't kill yourself to give it."

"She's just going through a lot. She just lost someone she loves in a very violent way," I murmur, but even as I say it, I'm not convinced that's what is going on. I don't think the police think that's all that's going on either, but despite looking extremely hard, they can't find proof to the contrary.

"Bullshit, Ellie," he all but snarls.

"What?" I ask, completely shocked. I know he's upset, but this...

"Your sister has always been like this. She acts like the world revolves around her and everyone is supposed to stop whatever they're doing to run to her aid."

"That's hardly fair considering what she's just been through, Liam."

"She got herself into a situation she never should have been in. If you expect me to feel pity for her, you better think again, Ice."

"I don't want to fight with you, Liam."

"I shouldn't have called. It's been a shit day and I knew better. I'm going to go, Ellie."

"Liam..."

"What?"

"Will you call me tomorrow?"

"Are you going to tell Harvey you're leaving next week?"

"Liam, please try to understand. I'm needed here."

"That's just it, Ellie. I do understand, you're trying to please everyone there, but you forgot one thing."

"What's that?"

"I need you, too, and if you love me, I should be a priority."

"It's all so black and white for you, isn't it Liam? You can't see my side at all. You expect me to just pack up and leave everything I have here. Yet, you aren't willing to do the same. It has to be all your way. You won't even think about compromising."

"Ellie—"

"I'll talk to you later," I respond, cutting him off. Then, I hang up.

My clock shows one in the morning before I realize that I'm crying...

DEVIL

"*K*illing me isn't going to bring your eye back."

Wolf's words are labored, slurred, and broken as he pants for air. I have to wonder if one of his broken ribs might have messed with his lung. Probably not, since he's still breathing. Sometimes, I think I keep waiting for him to die from my beatings to take the decision out of my hands of when I should end him.

I glance up at the clock and it's one in the morning. Another night where I'm late getting in bed with Torrent. That will probably lead to another fight. She knows what I'm doing. I haven't kept that from her. She told me she understands and I think she does. I can see the concern on her face, however, and each day that this drags on, that concern increases.

She's worried about me.

Hell, I'm worried about myself.

When I first got my hands on Wolf, I thought the darkness inside me had lifted. Now, it's becoming clearer that every day I spend breathing the same air as Wolf, feeds the darkness. Lately, I'm beginning to worry I'm losing sight of myself again.

"End this," Wolf says. He's not really begging, but he says it every night just the same. I never talk to him. He doesn't deserve my words. Instead, I do what I always do. I take the bat and slam it into the side of his face.

He's definitely not so pretty to look at now.

Wolf spits blood out of his mouth.

"End this," he demands again when he can recover enough to talk. I ignore him, just like always. Then, I take my knife and cut another couple of inches of skin off his leg.

It's a ritual I do every night before I leave and go jump in the shower. His leg looks disgusting now and is definitely infected, but that's just a small part of his worries. I throw the skin on the concrete floor for the rats to eat, knowing Wolf will be watching it. I want him to see that, to know that soon the rats will be feasting on his entire body.

"End this!" he yells again.

"Maybe tomorrow," I reply, giving him hope. Hell, maybe I'm giving it to myself. I know that the sooner this is over, the sooner I can get on with my life and enjoy Torrent's love and that of our son. Logically, I know it, but yet I can't make myself stop torturing him. I keep thinking I'll get to a point where I feel that the score is even.

It never is.

What's that old adage? An eye for an eye? Maybe tomorrow I'll try cutting out both of Wolf's eyes with a dull knife. Maybe that will make me feel like the score has been settled. It could happen...

But I doubt it.

ELLIE

"I think it's finally over."

"It sounded like it," I agree, watching my sister carefully.

"Thank God. Now, I can get on with my life."

"We should start planning Glenna's memorial service," I agree. "It's kind of sad that she had no family, nothing in this world."

"I'm not giving her a memorial service," Dawn announces.

"You're not?"

I should probably be surprised, but I'm not. My sister and I have always been different, but in the last few weeks I've started wondering if I knew her at all. We just got done with another interview with the lead detectives in the case. Although, it wasn't really an interview as much as it was an interrogation. They think my sister helped Wolf. They think she's hiding him. Now, I obviously know she's not doing that, but I agree with the detective. Dawn knows more than she's telling us. I don't suppose it matters anymore, however. They're moving Glenna's case from priority. They're focusing on their hunt for Wolf, and I doubt they'll ever completely stop that—especially after I supplied them with his real name by lying and telling them that he approached me in the bar first with his real name and that I had no idea he was talking to my sister or Glenna under a different name. They'll never find Wolf, however, and of that I'm certain. That means, for my sister, it's over. It should be a time of joy, but with Glenna dead, Liam so far away and not really talking to me, there's not much joy to be found.

"No, I've already spoken to the funeral home. Once Glenna's body is released, I'm having her cremated quietly with her ashes scattered," Dawn says.

"Shouldn't we have a small service?" I ask.

"Don't pressure your sister, Ellie. If she doesn't want a service for this girl, she doesn't need to do one. There's no point. You said yourself that the girl didn't really have anyone. She was alone in this world. The world is for the living. Dawn needs to put this behind her."

I stop walking towards the car. I look at my mother and sister and I wonder—not for the first time—who they are. Did they change overnight into these people, or were they like this all along and I blindly went along not noticing until I found out they had lied to me.

"Well? Are you coming? Dawn and I need to get back to Page."

"You're going home to Page?" I ask, blindsided. This is the first I'm hearing about Dawn going back with Mom. "I thought you were having Glenna cremated and you both said you'd help me finish packing and closing down the house. You never mentioned leaving."

"The world doesn't revolve around you, Eleanor," Mom snaps.

"I'm having Glenna's body transferred to the funeral home in Page. They'll do it there and it will be half the cost."

"I... You two have been talking about this for a while," I stutter, feeling kind of stupid. All this time, I thought Dawn just wasn't talking to me. I assumed that she was just closed up because of the trauma. That obviously wasn't it. She's been talking quite a bit to our mother, apparently.

"So? What does it matter?"

"It doesn't, I guess."

"You don't need us to pack up. If you're intent to go back to that biker and ruin your life, then do it. You won't listen to me, you never did," Mom says, her voice full of annoyance and derision.

"Liam won't ruin my life, Mom. He loves me."

"He's nothing but a criminal. I've seen those biker shows on television. He's a thug that makes his money dealing in drugs and women. Why you want that element in your life, Eleanor is beyond me. I had hoped that when you came home the first time, you'd gotten smart, but apparently, I was wrong."

"That's not who Liam is. You're basing your hate of him on a dramatized television show," I respond. My voice is monotone, because I'm not sure what I'm feeling. I just know that I feel like I never knew my family at all.

"Don't you try and defend him to me. Dawn and I both saw how broken you were when you came home."

"Yeah, Ellie. Maybe you've forgotten what a mess you were that first month when Fury didn't even bother to call you. It was five weeks before he finally worried about you. *Five*. You want to act like he's such a good guy. He's scum," Dawn snarls and I step back, because the hate in her eyes is so deep that it's terrifying. I don't think it's all directed at Liam. I think it just lives in her.

"Funny, you want to call him scum and Mom wants to talk about the things he is supposedly involved in and yet both of you are happy he'll be taking care of Wolf's body. How many times have you quizzed me about that, Dawn? You want to make sure he's dead and never found again. Isn't that right?" I ask her, paraphrasing the small conversations that we've had when it came to Wolf.

"Wolf was a monster, he deserved to die," Mom sniffs, but Dawn just stares at me. I think we're beginning to understand each other.

"At least on that we can agree," I murmur. "While you two are busy judging my husband—"

"He's not your husband anymore. You should have put that mistake behind you. You knew he was bad then, or you wouldn't have come home," Mom snaps. "Why my girls are intent on ruining their lives over trash, I don't know. Thank God that Dawn has finally seen the light. I'm giving up hope on you."

I flinch. Not so much at what my mother just said, more because she's almost right. I did come home because of Liam's life. I didn't trust his love for me.

"I would have went back to him, then. I just needed time to sort through all of the sadness. I would have gone back to him if you'd told me he called."

"And that's exactly why we didn't," Mom yells. The words are so loud that I know the people on the street are now staring at us. I shake my head. I thought going back home to Page back then was going home to my safe zone. I thought I could go there and think things over then Liam would call and we'd be able to fix things between us. I can see the exact moment everything began to go off the rails and it's all pointing at me. I have more of Dawn and my mother in me than I realized and suddenly, I know that's not a good thing.

I turn away from them, walking the opposite direction.

"Where are you going?" Dawn yells.

"Home," I tell them without looking back. I don't owe them anything. They're not the people I had built up in my mind. They're toxic. I made the wrong decisions when I left Tennessee. I need to learn from them and make sure I don't repeat the same ones.

I just hope I'm not too late.

FURY

"How are you doing, Fury?" Diesel asks, coming over to sit with me.

It's a quiet night at the club. I think we're all starting to worry about Devil. He's still got Wolf locked in the basement. The guy is breathing, but it's beyond me how. With all of the wounds he has and blood loss, he should be dead. I guess that's the thing about monsters, they wouldn't be scary if they did what was expected of them. And Wolf? He's definitely a monster.

"I'm okay. Got a lot of shit on my mind," I mumble. "Where's Devil?"

"You know where he is," Diesel mutters.

"Yeah, I do."

We both look over at Torrent. She's sitting talking to Dani and Crusher, but even from this distance I can see the circles under her eyes. She's worried about her man, just like we all are.

"Are we going to have to intervene?" I ask Diesel. He lets out a loud sigh that makes it clear he's as worried as the rest of us.

"I hate to. God knows that Devil deserves this. I can't imagine all of the hell he went through. I even got my turn at Wolf, but Devil..." he shifts his shoulders a minute before continuing.

"There are things he needs to work through. If he doesn't get his head together soon, I'll step in and send in the big guns."

"What's that mean?"

"I'll send Torrent down there to talk some sense into him. She's been letting him fight his demons as best as he can, but she's almost at the end of her rope, too."

"He won't thank you for letting Torrent anywhere near that fucker again, even if he is chained up like a side of beef in a packing plant."

"Maybe not, but it might take that to pull Devil's head out of his ass," Diesel says and he's not wrong.

"Women have a way of doing that. Diesel, I need to talk to you."

"When are you leaving?" he asks, smirking.

"What?"

"You're going to tell me you are going to go back to Phoenix, right?"

I let out a laugh, which isn't of humor, rather, it's one of respect. I should have known that Diesel would know where my head is. There's a reason he makes a damn good president of our crew.

"I have to, Brother. I've lived without her for almost two years. I did it, but it was miserable. Since having her back in my life, being without her again feels like I'm fucking dying."

"Are you coming back?" he asks and that's the part that kills me.

"I want to," I tell him.

"But, you're not sure she will."

"There were things she didn't like me doing for the club," I tell him, tiptoeing over a touchy subject and hoping to leave it at that.

"Like going after Vicki."

"Yeah."

"I always wondered if that wasn't the real reason she left. It happened when you left to hunt that bitch down the first time."

"It was part of it, yeah, but our problems were bigger than that, Diesel, man. We needed to work through shit and instead..."

"Ellie left."

"And I didn't try to go to her when I got back. I let my pride get in my way," I admit.

"Pride is a hard thing for a man to let go of and sometimes he shouldn't. It's what makes us the men we are, the men that can live this life that we lead," he says. I nod my head, because he's right. "It makes a piss-poor bed fellow, though," he says with a grin, holding his glass up in salute. I clink mine against his, swallowing down the whiskey, as we share a drink and understanding. Diesel gets up, slaps me on the shoulder and gives me the words I need. "Do what you need to do, Fury. You know this is your home. We're always here for you, however you need us."

"I do. I just know that Ellie is my life. Without her—"

The front door opens, I barely look up, figuring it's one of the pledges or club candy. But, my eye catches that long wave of blonde hair and I do a double-take.

Standing at the door is Ellie...suitcase in hand.

ELLIE

I nervously stand at the door and I know all eyes are on me. I can feel them. I keep my gaze concentrated on Liam though. I'm so nervous, I feel like a cat on a hot tin roof. I'm praying that just showing up was the right choice. Liam could have already decided he was tired of putting up with me. Until I was faced with my mother and sister on the streets in Phoenix, I honestly didn't realize that my first instinct was to run when things got difficult, but it is. Maybe I have more of my father in me than I realized. He sure ran from our family. Now that I see my mother without blinders, I can only imagine how difficult his life was.

"Ice," Fury growls, coming towards me. His big muscular body charges at me like a bull and I'm starting to rethink the red dress I'm wearing.

I gasp as he pulls me into his arms. My suitcase drops to the floor, as he slams his mouth down against mine, kissing me so hard that it takes my breath away.

"Liam," I moan, as we break apart. I can hear the club behind us, catcalling and yelling out, but they seem a world away. I'm pressed against Liam, my arms around his shoulders, my legs wrapped around his hips. I'm looking into his gray eyes, the taste of him on my lips.

"You're here," he growls, his fingers biting into the flesh of my ass, as he grinds me against him. His dick is pushing against his jeans.

"I'm here."

"Thank fuck. Tell me you're here to stay, Ellie."

"I'm here for as long as you want me, Liam," I respond, wondering if he catches what I said. I know I'm going to have to come clean to him and there's a chance he may never forgive me.

"Always, Ice, always," he growls, taking my mouth again.

I know we're walking, and I can hear the crowd's voices in the main room get dimmer, but it doesn't matter. I drink in the reality of being in Liam's arms again, of having his kiss, of feeling his arms around me. I've been so empty since he left Phoenix, that I can barely believe this is happening.

He takes us to his room. A room that used to be ours. I'm surprised that it hasn't changed, but literally nothing has changed —including the fact that our wedding photo is still on the dresser. When he puts me down, I walk over to it, picking it up.

Our smiling faces are reflected back at me. It was over four years ago, but we look so much younger and carefree. We lost our way. To realize that most of that fault lies on my shoulders, is a hard pill to swallow. Liam never changed. He was who he was when I married him. I was young and naïve. A virgin who romanticized what our life would be like.

I was so wrong.

But, the one thing I wasn't wrong about was the fact that Liam loved me. He has always loved me.

"We need to talk," Liam says. I slowly raise my gaze to look at him through the reflection in the mirror, our wedding photo still in my hand.

"We do," I admit, nervously. I have so much to tell him, so much to confess. What happens if he hates me for it?"

"It will have to wait until after I have you, Ellie."

"Liam, there are things you need to know. Things we really should discuss before—"

"Nothing you have to say is going to change the fact that you belong to me, Ellie. We'll talk about it all, but it will be after."

"After..." I murmur, the heated look in his eyes is so hot it feels as if it might scorch me.

"Definitely after. Now, put your hands on the dresser and spread your legs apart," he orders, my body shivers in response.

Maybe I'm weak. Maybe I should try to make him listen to me, but I don't. I put our photo down and I grip the dresser, positioning my legs wider to make room for him. He comes up behind, his large body making me feel small and feminine. His ink covered hand comes down to grab our wedding photo.

"You kept it," I murmur, because the significance of that isn't lost on me.

"Always," he says. "Just because you left, Ellie, didn't mean it was over for me. I love you. I'll always love you." I want to believe that's true, I pray it is. I close my eyes as he nuzzles my neck, putting whisper-soft kisses there, his beard teasing my skin. "I'll just put this over here, where it's safe. I don't want it to break as I'm slamming into you," he purrs against my ear.

"Liam..."

"This isn't going to be slow and easy, Ellie. It's been too long. I'm going to fuck you so hard that your legs give out," he promises, as he puts our picture on the small stool beside the dresser. Then, I feel his hands at the zipper of my dress.

We'll have to talk later. Right now, I just want to get lost in Liam's touch.

"I don't want slow and easy, Liam. I just want you, anyway I can get you," I tell him and as he releases my zipper, I'm filled with anticipation.

ELLIE

$\mathcal{A}$s my dress falls to the floor, I'm left in nothing more than my thong and matching bra. Liam's hand moves over my back, slowly followed by his lips, kissing a path that only he knows—that only he has explored. His hand dips down, moving over my ass cheek, squeezing the fleshy globe, once…twice and then, without warning, smacking it. I cry out, not prepared, even though I should have been.

"I've missed this ass, Ellie. Who does it belong to, baby?"

"You, Liam. Always, you," I answer immediately.

"Such a good little girl, giving me the right answer. I think maybe you need a reward." His fingertip moves along the fabric of my thong and it seems to burn me as it does. "What do you think, Ice? Do you need a reward?"

"Please, Liam," I beg, so turned on it's ridiculous and he's barely touched me. His fingers slide under the fabric of my thong and he pulls it tight so that it puts friction against my pussy and slips between my lips abrading my clit and causing me to moan at the sensation. He pulls the fabric outward, tugging on it so it works my pussy like a puppet. My clit, already swollen, is

i

drenched, and I'm sure the fabric is too. "Oh fuck," I hiss, thinking he's going to make me come using nothing but my panties.

"Lean down and angle that sweet little ass out, Ellie," he growls against my ear.

I shudder, so close to exploding that if he just touched me I'd shatter. I do exactly as he asks, afraid that if I don't he'll stop and that's the last thing I want.

He does stop, but even as I whimper in protest, I hear the fabric of my thong rip.

"Liam, you're torturing me," I complain. I hold tighter onto the dresser, afraid my knees are going to give out on me.

I look into the mirror. His head is bent down and I know he's looking at his cock, but I can't see from this angle. His face is almost tortured and beautiful in its hunger. I bite into my lip, my eyes closing as I feel the head of his heated cock move over my ass, leaving a wet trail where he spanked me.

"Fuck, yeah, Ice. I really did miss this ass," he groans.

"Liam..."

I don't know what I'm asking for, maybe nothing. I just know whatever he's doing to me seems monumental. Intuitively, I know that I'll never be the same again. I feel the head of his cock push between my cheeks, applying pressure to the entrance of my ass. My body betrays me, automatically thrusting out to meet him, wanting what he's giving, even if I'm apprehensive. He moves his cock back and forth in between the small valley, pushing his head against the tight opening, but never quite entering. He does this repeatedly, and I get lost in the repetition. Then, unexpectedly, his cock moves lower, tunneling between my thighs, and sliding against the tender aroused flesh that leads to my clit.

"You're so fucking wet, Ice. I'd forgotten what magic we create together."

He's right. That's the only word for it, too.

Magic.

"Quit torturing me, Liam. I need you," I pant, leaning deeper against the dresser, I reach my hand between my legs, to touch his wet cock, pressing it up against me, loving the way that feels. Liam slaps my ass, this time harder than before, causing my entire body to shudder and a fresh new wave of wetness to soak his cock and run down my thighs.

I've never been this wet in my life.

"Remember the rules, Ellie. What are they?"

"You give me what I need and how I need it," I murmur the words that I learned early on in our relationship. Liam is definitely the dominate man in the bedroom and I love every second of it.

His hand wraps in my hair, as he twists the curls and roughly pulls my head back.

"I hope you're ready for me, Ice," he growls, slamming inside of me and not stopping until he's completely ceded. It's rough enough that it takes my breath away, but it feels so good that I'm instantly squeezing my muscles against his cock, trying to keep him inside of me. "Jesus, Ellie," he groans. "It gets better every time." He begins sliding in and out of me. His strokes hard, methodical, and soul-rocking.

"God, yes, Liam. More, baby. I'm so close. Take me harder," I yell, and I am yelling. I've never been quiet in the bedroom. Nothing Liam does to me has ever made being quiet an option.

Somehow, impossibly, his thrusts get harder, more controlled, but there's no doubt that he's drilling my pussy. His hand tightens in my hair.

"Is this what you wanted, Ellie? You wanted me to fuck you so hard you'll be sore for days?"

"You're mine, Ellie," he growls, withdrawing only to slam all the way back in again. "Say it."

"Yours, Liam."

He reaches around me and I feel his fingers slide against my clit as he slams in and out of me. He's fucking me so hard the dresser is moving with each thrust. His forceful grip on me will leave bruises, but I welcome them.

"Come for me, Ellie. I want to feel you come all over my cock as I empty my cum inside of you."

That's all it takes. I literally combust, coming so hard, that I worry I'm going to pass out. I feel Liam's cum inside of me, stream after stream, filling me so full that it leaks out and I love it. I close my eyes, celebrating the fact that I belong to Liam once again. Whatever else is wrong, one thing will always be true.

I really do belong to him.

ELLIE

$\mathcal{I}$ wake slowly, stretching the kinks out of my well used body. I lost count of the number of times Liam made me come last night. I'm pretty sure I begged him to stop that last time and then threatened to kill him when he did. The memory brings a smile to my face.

I'm alone in bed, I know that at once, because I instantly miss Liam. It's nothing unusual. He always leaves early to get started on his day with his brothers. Besides, it's almost eleven. I never sleep this late. My only excuse is that I'm exhausted from all of his attention last night.

Part of me dreads today, because I know that Liam and I will have to talk. I don't know how that will go, but I have to believe as much as we love one another that we can survive it. Surely the fact that in all this time he's never had another woman, and keeps our wedding photo on the dresser, means that he feels the same way I do.

"About time you woke up, lazy bones."

I grin, as I look over to Liam, who opens the door and comes in carrying a tray.

"I had a man who wore me out all night."

"He sounds like a keeper," Liam jokes.

"Definitely," I answer. "I don't plan on ever letting him go."

He puts a knee on the bed and leans down to kiss me. It's a brief kiss and I want more, but he pulls away and settles in behind me, after fixing the tray in front of me.

"Brought you breakfast in bed to keep your strength up," he says, kissing the side of my neck.

I lean back against him, my head tilted to give access, and I breathe him and this moment in.

"I thought you'd be busy with the club this morning," I tell him. "This is a good surprise."

"Your first day back, Ice? You aren't going to find me anywhere but right where I'm at."

"You're going to spoil me."

I'm looking at the eggs, bacon, toast and fruit he's brought, but that's not what I'm talking about.

"That's the plan, baby. I have the whole day to spend with you. What would you like to do?"

"This is nice."

"What?" he asks, distractedly, his fingers sifting through my hair.

I angle so I can see him and take the strip of bacon I'm holding and offer him a bite. He leans in to take a bite. I'm mesmerized by the movement of his mouth, his lips and the strong set of his jawline. My man is truly beautiful. He'd hate me for saying that, but he totally is.

"Staying with you in bed all day." I grin up at him, not even kidding. "That sounds like a perfect day to me."

"That could be arranged," he murmurs, reaching around me to swipe a grape from the fruit on my plate. "Of course, I have one small request," he says, putting the grape to my mouth. I suck it inside and he pushes his thumb between my lips. I see that familiar heat back in his eyes.

"What's that?" I ask, suddenly feeling warm and flushed all over.

"Throw out your birth control, Ice."

My body goes solid for a minute.

"Wh..." I have to stop and catch my breath. "What?"

"Throw out your birth control," he says kissing along my shoulder.

"Liam, what are you saying?" I ask, wondering why it feels like there's this gigantic elephant sitting on my chest. It literally hurts to breathe.

"I want to make babies with you, Ice."

"I...I'm not ready for that, Liam," I tell him, and instantly, he changes. I can feel the tension in the room go solid.

"You always wanted kids, Ellie. You once told me you wanted a house full of them."

"I was young, Liam. I didn't fully understand life and what we would face."

"But you do now?"

"Not all, but I know enough that a house full of kids is not practical," I tell him, my heart hurting with the words.

"Don't try telling Dani and Crusher that," he growls and I frown.

"Liam, I'm not saying I don't ever want kids. I just don't want them right now. You and I just found our way back to each other. Can't we enjoy that and find solid ground, before we think about kids? Besides who's to say I won't have trouble having children again? We need to think about things carefully."

"I didn't know we weren't on solid ground, Ellie."

"I didn't mean it like that, Liam. Please, don't be upset with me. I just need some time," I plead and slowly I feel some of the tension leave him—although not completely.

"We're not talking about never having kids, though. Right, Ice?"

"Right," I tell him. "I just want time alone with you for now. We need time for us to find our way back to each other in every way, first. That's not too much to ask, is it?"

I'm letting my panic, lead my mouth. Everything I'm saying is the truth, just not all of it. How do I tell him, I'm scared there will come a day when he might not want me? How do I tell him that just the subject of children makes me nervous?

"I guess I can live with that and besides, there's a bonus," he says, moving the tray to a nightstand. For a minute, I zone out, staring at the tray, sitting precariously at an angle. It seems to represent how my life feels right now. Like I'm on the edge of a cliff and nearing disaster.

"There is?" I ask, turning my gaze back to Liam, while summoning up a smile, even though smiling is the last thing I really want to do right now.

"We can practice making babies in the meantime," he says and then he kisses me.

I take his kiss, losing myself in the pleasure of his touch and the magical things he does to my body. I know I promised myself that I would talk to him today, but it can't hurt to put it off for another day or so. Right now, I just want to remind Liam—remind us both—how good things are when we're together.

FURY

 *ne Week Later*

I LOOK over at the girls laughing and talking and my heart squeezes seeing Ellie happy and laughing. She's been back a week now and having her back is better than I imagined. Despite how great it's been though, I know there's something going on with her. People change, I get that, but Ellie is reserved in a way she never was before. She's cautious and there are dark circles under her eyes. Something is going on with her, but I can't put my finger on it. There's a chance I'm just looking for something to be wrong because I finally have everything I want, but I don't think that's it.

"You look like a man with a lot on your mind," Connie says, coming up behind me and moving her hand along my back. I take a step away from her.

"Get out of here, Connie. You know you're barking up the wrong tree. Ellie's back."

"Just because she's back, that doesn't mean you and I can't still party."

"It means that and more."

"I'm so sick of you guys. You think we're good to use until you get you a *good* woman. They aren't any different than the rest of us you know. They put their pants on one leg at a time and their shit still stinks."

"The difference is I love her. Are we going to have issues here?" I ask her, narrowing my eyes at her. I don't need this bullshit.

"No trouble here. She'll fly the coop again and you'll be looking for me. Don't worry, lover, I'll be here. You, me, Nancy and Scorpion can all play like we used to."

"You need to go. I'm only going to say this once, Connie. You stay away from Ellie. I trust you understand me."

I watch as her face twists unhappily, her lips purse. I think she's about to mouth off. She doesn't. She walks away, but she's clearly not happy.

"What was that about?" Ellie asks, coming over.

"No idea," I grumble, lying through my teeth. "Probably sees you're back and wants to cause trouble."

That part at least isn't a lie.

"Maybe I need to have a word with her," Ellie says, curling into my side. I wrap my arm around her and kiss the top of her head.

"Just let it go, Ellie. She'll soon see you're here to stay and that you're all I need. Then, she'll go back to the other brothers."

"If you say so." She lets out a sad sigh and I turn her so I can see her face, because I don't want her worried about Connie, or anyone for that matter. "Torrent is worried," she finally says. I breathe a little easier with the change of subject.

"I know. Devil's back down there tonight, isn't he?"

"Yeah. Will he listen to you, if you try and get him to end all of this?"

"I don't know, Ice. Diesel is thinking about sending Torrent down and confronting him so that Devil is forced to face everything."

"Shit," Ellie hisses.

"Yeah."

"That won't be easy for Torrent."

"I know, but there might not be a way around it."

"They've had so much pain. I mean I wasn't around to see it, but just hearing about it now breaks my heart. It just seems like such a waste that Devil still has to suffer now that it could all be over."

"He'll be okay, Ellie. He just was put through hell. It's going to take him a while to get it straightened out in his head, you know?"

"I hope you're right," Ellie murmurs.

I hope I am, too...

TORRENT

$\mathcal{W}$ alking down the dark stairway is not my favorite. It brings back memories I don't want. My nose curls at the smell and I stop, unsure if I can go through with this. I know Diesel thought it would be the only way Logan would discuss things with me, but God...

"St...op."

The voice is hoarse, almost unrecognizable, but I know it at once.

I take a few more steps, still afraid, but needing to do this. I want my husband back.

I need him back.

"Logan?" I whisper tentatively, as I round the corner.

"Torrent, get the fuck out of here," Logan growls, his voice sounding inhuman, as he talks to me in a way that he hasn't before.

"Tor—"

"You don't say her name!" Logan screams out, as he takes a large, gruesome looking bat and swings it into Wolf's body.

"Logan, honey...."

"Get the fuck out of here! He doesn't get to hear you. He doesn't get to see you again."

I look up at the misshapen body, hanging by chains from a hook. I hold my stomach as nausea threatens to rise.

"Sweetheart, I don't think he can see anything anymore," I murmur. Wolf's face has oversized bandages over his eyes. I don't know what Devil has done—but from the dark red traces of blood that show under the gauze, I can guess.

"God, Angel, just go. I'll be up soon."

"I can't do that," I tell him. Wolf is moaning, but I think Devil's hits have made it so that he can't talk to me, and for that I'm glad.

"You need to go, Torrent."

"I'm not leaving without you, Logan. We're a team, remember?"

"I'll be up when I'm done."

He sounds so tortured that tears begin falling from my eyes, I can't stop them and I don't even try.

"When are you going to be done, Logan?"

"I don't know," he responds, sounding lost.

I walk over to him, ignoring the blood that is splattered on his clothes. I know that I need to reach Logan.

"I'm so sorry, Logan. I'm so very sorry." I go up on my tiptoes, putting a hand on each side of his face and forcing him to look at me and focus.

"Why are you sorry, Angel?"

"This is all my fault. I should have seen through Wolf, I should have left with you and stopped fighting. I did this to you," I tell him, the tears falling harder as I finally confess my biggest regret, the pain I try to keep hidden, and the guilt that has always festered inside of me.

"You didn't do this to me, Angel. You saved me," Logan says, letting the bat drop to the floor. His arms go around me then, holding me.

"I brought Wolf into your life. If it hadn't been for me..."

"If it wasn't for you, I'd be dead."

"I think you're forgetting that I'm the reason you were hurt in the first place."

"I'd do it all again, Angel. I'd do it every fucking day, over and over, if it meant that I get to live my life with you. You are everything and now we have Cannon and any brothers and sisters we give him. I'd do it all again if my reward is the life we have now, Angel."

"If that's true, then why are you down here instead of upstairs tucking our boy in and making love to me in our bed?"

"I want to make him pay."

"Sweetheart, you have. Send him to hell and be done with it. Put him behind us."

"Torrent, you don't understand."

"I understand that as long as you do this, you're letting him take more from us. You're feeding the guilt I have, the pain you have, and you're letting him breathe the same air our little boy does. It's time to let go of the past, Logan. We both have to."

"Killing him would be doing him a favor. He doesn't deserve that."

"I think killing him will make it so he can't be this shadow over us anymore. Gunner talked to Rayne and she wants us to come out so I can meet her. I want you by my side. I don't want to go to bed at night and wonder when you will be there. I want you with me."

"But I'll be giving him what he wants," Logan argues.

"He'll be dead and no one will be left to mourn him. We'll be happy, we'll have sex like rabbits and have a houseful of kids, Logan. We'll enjoy family Christmases, full of laughter and love. That's our revenge, baby. We'll live and we'll make beautiful memories. We'll grow old together. We'll have all the good and he'll be dead and forgotten."

"I love you, Angel."

"Then come back upstairs. End all of this and let's get on with being happy," I tell him, begging and praying I'm reaching him.

"Go on up. I'll be there in a bit," he says and I feel deflated. I thought he might listen to me...

"But, Logan—"

"I'll end it and get rid of him. Then, I'll come home to you," he promises. I stretch to kiss him on the lips—just a brief touch.

"Don't be long, please? I need my husband, I've been without him for far too long."

"I'll make it quick."

"I love you, Logan."

"Love you, too, Torrent."

"You promise you're okay?"

"I'm better and I'll get the rest of the way with your help," he tells me, his voice still sad, but much less bleak.

"You always have that."

"I know that, Angel. I definitely know that."

I walk away, after giving his hand a squeeze. I stop midway on the steps and wait. I'm not sure what I'm waiting for, but I still do it.

"I've never been a religious man, but I really fucking hope there is a hell. Because tonight, while I'm putting a baby inside of Torrent, the only thing that will bring me more pleasure is to know that while I'm doing that, you're in that fucking lake of fire they talk about, dying over and over," he says.

There's the sound of a bullet that has been muffled and then another. It keeps going and I figure he's emptying an entire round, but I walk toward the door.

It's over.

ELLIE

"*H*ave you seen, Liam?" I ask Torrent. "I woke up and he was gone. He didn't mention having to go anywhere today, but I can't find him anywhere."

I'm trying not to panic, I've yet to really talk to him and as each day passes, I know I have to. I just haven't been able to drum up my courage just yet.

"He left early. Logan needed him to help him...dispose of something."

"Does that mean it's finally finished?"

"Yeah," she says softly.

"Is Devil okay?" I ask, not wanting to pry, but I've always loved Devil. He's like that annoying big brother that you love even when you want to choke him.

"I think he will be. He seemed better last night after he...you know."

"I know," I respond. First rule of old ladies everywhere, you never speak aloud the crimes your men might commit. There are ears everywhere. "I'm just about to go and get some lunch. Want to go with me?"

i

"Sure, I just put Cannon down for his nap. Shit. Logan has me calling him that now," Torrent mutters, making me laugh.

"It's a good road name," I say with a giggle.

"It is, but never tell Logan I admitted to that."

"Your secret is safe with me." I'm laughing as we enter the kitchen, but when we get there and Connie is there with another girl that I don't know, the laugh dies. I don't like that she approached Liam last night. I know Liam told me to forget it, but that's not easy. You have to handle these things head on, or bitches like Connie think they have the green light to fuck your man. I don't think Liam would jeopardize us like that, but I don't like Connie thinking that's okay.

I follow Torrent to the bar. We walk past Connie and the other girl and though Connie's eyes bore into me, she doesn't say anything. I sit down at the bar and grab a paper plate. There's large platters full of lunch meat and condiments. There's loaves of bread at the end of that. One great thing about club life is that there is always ready prepared food. It works great for me because I truly hate cooking.

The entire time Torrent and I are constructing our sandwiches, I feel Connie's eyes on me. With each passing moment, it sparks my anger.

"Jesus."

"What's wrong?" Torrent asks, looking up at me in surprise.

"Some problem with the club candy. She hit on Liam last night and he shot her down. Now she's staring me down. Liam asked me not to talk to her and to just let it go. He thinks that she'll get the message when it becomes clearer that I'm here to stay."

"Damn it. Men can be so clueless," Torrent snorts.

"Right?"

"Is it Connie the Cunt? Girl, a house could fall on her and she still couldn't find a damn clue. I thought we were rid of her once, but she came back after begging to Rory that she was homeless.

Rory has a big heart and I'm pretty sure she was on an overdose of pregnancy hormones," Torrent mutters.

I nearly choke on my sandwich. "Connie the Cunt? Now, that's hilarious."

"And true, don't forget that part," Torrent giggles with me. It is funny, but I wish Rory hadn't let Connie come back.

"What are you two laughing at?" Connie calls out and we both stop laughing. It appears Connie is going to demand a showdown after all.

"Did anyone talk to you, Connie? It's not your business to know or even care what I'm laughing about," I tell her, dropping my sandwich back on my plate and crossing my arms at my waist. I didn't like Connie much when I lived here before and now, I *really* don't like her.

"You always did think you were hot stuff, Eleanor. But, you're not. You're shit. You got such a big head because you were one of the original old ladies. Well, times have changed since you've been gone. In case you haven't realized it, there's more women here now, and you're no longer the queen around here."

"I'm happy with the way things are, Connie. And any way you look at it, I will always mean more around here than you, so don't you worry about my ego."

"Bitch. Why do you think you mean more to the club than me? I've had almost every man here. They want anything I give them."

"Jesus, Connie, you act like it's a big thing to spread your legs for a man. Men are like pigs. They see a cheap puddle of mud they'll rut in it all day, but it's not because they give a fuck about the water," Torrent says, giving me a wink and taking a bite of her sandwich.

"What are you talking about?" Connie demands.

"Stop trying to explain. Sarcasm goes straight over her head. Too much hair dye," I tell Torrent, quickly growing bored with this conversation.

"Oh yeah, bitch? You think you're so great, but you'll be gone again soon and when you do, I'll be there to make sure Fury is taken care of."

"Now, you're dreaming," I tell her, shaking my head. "Liam can't stand you. He'd never touch you, even if I wasn't in the picture and trust me when I tell you, Connie, I'm not going anywhere. Liam is mine and that's not about to change."

"Keep believing that. Fury will come find me. I know how he likes it."

"Whatever," I mutter. "I've suddenly lost my appetite," I tell Torrent.

"Can't say as I blame you. She's forgotten her place."

"My place? What the fuck do you know what my place is?"

"I know that talking to old ladies at all puts you in jeopardy but disrespecting us will get you kicked out," Torrent warns.

"You can try. Won't change the fact that I've had your man's dick and Fury's. That's really what pisses you two off," Connie snarls.

"Bitch please, you haven't touched Logan's cock, or if you have, it was before he met me. You're just an annoying gnat."

"Maybe I haven't, but I sure as hell have had Fury's."

My heart freezes in my chest and I know the shock shows on my face, it caught me too unaware. I didn't get time to disguise it.

"That surprises you, doesn't it, Eleanor? I gave your man what you couldn't when you left. So go ahead, play old lady until you grow bored. When you leave again, I'll be here to pick up the pieces, just like last time."

"Ellie—" Torrent says, putting her hand on mine.

"You get around Liam and I'll kill you," I tell her and right now, I don't think I'm kidding.

"You can try, but I know I can handle your skinny ass," Connie says and she spits in the air at my direction.

That's what it takes to flip my switch. I probably should walk away, but the thought of Liam fucking this woman—not to mention lying to me about it—pushes me over the edge. I launch myself at her, grabbing some of her cheap, dyed hair and shoving her onto the floor.

"What the fuck is going on here?" Diesel growls. I hear him, but I don't look at him, I'm too busy trying to yank enough hair out of Connie's head to make the bitch bald. I'm wailing at her with my fists and my nails when Diesel wraps his arms around me, pulling me off of Connie.

"Let me go. I'm going to teach this bitch some respect," I growl, kicking to get free.

Rebel pulls Connie away.

"Bitch!" Connie snarls.

"Whore!" I scream back.

"Scorp, track Fury down and tell him he needs to get back here and contain his woman."

"Contain me? What about that piece of trash?" I bark, still trying to get free.

"I'll deal with her," Diesel says. "She's out of here."

"Why? She started this shit!" Connie screams.

"You spit on her. Number one rule for all the girls here is that you don't disrespect old ladies. You know that shit Connie, and you still try to push it. Now, I'm done," Diesel growls. "I should have never let your ass back in here after I kicked you out the first time. You managed to beg to Rory and she allowed you to come back. I still haven't figured out how you managed that shit."

I calm down, somewhat then. What he says makes me feel marginally better. "You can let me go. I'll behave now," I tell Diesel and he lets me go.

That was his mistake.

The second he lets me go, I go after her again and this time my fist connects with her face. It hurts like hell, but the satisfaction is well worth it, even when she hits me back, and manages to cut my cheek with her fake ass diamond. I yank a big gob of her hair out and it's still in my hand when Diesel drags me away again.

Still worth it.

ELLIE

"What the fuck is going on, Ellie?" Fury growls, storming into our room.

A room I've been locked in for the last hour.

Diesel practically threw me in here and then locked me in. I didn't even know these rooms could be locked from the outside. That's a bunch of bullshit. If I was going to stay here—which I'm not—that would have to change.

My suitcase is on the bed and I'm throwing things in it. I've only been packing the last fifteen minutes. Until that time, I was trying to break out of the room. When it became clear that wasn't happening, I started packing.

"I tell you what's going on, *Liam*," I snarl. "Connie the mother-trucking biker slut."

"Fuck," Liam hisses and my heart squeezes in my damn chest. Until this moment, I expected him to completely deny everything, but he's not. When I look at him and really focus, I see the guilt on his face.

"Right," I mutter, throwing more shit in my suitcase. "I'm such a fucking idiot. I truly believed you."

"Damn it, Ellie."

"How many more were there, Liam?"

"Ellie—"

"Never mind, don't tell me. It's not like I'd believe you anyway. I'm such a stupid fool. Why did I believe you? *My dick has never been inside another woman, Ellie. I only wanted you, Ellie. My dick was broken without you, Ellie.* Jesus! I'm a fucking idiot!" I snarl, again throwing more crap in my suitcase.

Liam stomps over to the bed, grabs my suitcase, holding it upside down so everything falls onto the floor. Then, he slings the suitcase across the room.

"You're not leaving, Ellie!"

"The fuck I'm not, Liam. There's nothing keeping me here."

"Damn it, woman! I'm here. I matter. Didn't you learn the first time around?" he growls. I pick up my suitcase, looking at his face. I hate that superior look he's sporting. I swing the suitcase at him, hitting him in the waist. Not that the big dummy could feel it.

"I really hate that you're built like a brick outhouse."

"That's not the term, Ellie."

"I don't give a fuck, Liam. You lied to me."

"I didn't. I just didn't tell you the whole truth."

"Are you for real right now? Do you know how it felt to be told by a whore that she's been riding your dick for two years!?!?!"

"First of all, that bitch hasn't been riding my dick. I didn't lie to you when I said my cock hasn't been inside another woman."

"Then tell me, how does that whore claim she's had your cock? Don't you try lying to me either, Liam. You have guilt written all over your freaking face."

"The bitch sucked me off a few times, Ellie. That's it."

"That's it? Christ you're such an asshole. That's why you told me you got a clean bill of health before coming to Phoenix. I'm so stupid. I should have known it happened before. I mean, you were getting a hummer at the bar. Gee, Liam, I knew you liked blowjobs, but I didn't know it was your favorite."

"That's because with you, it's not," he growls.

"Oh, I'm so sorry I don't live up to the skills of a fucking professional. Shit, you've been fucking me without a raincoat! If you gave me a fucking disease, I'll kill you, Liam Maverick."

"I don't have anything. You know as well as I do that the club makes the girls take mandatory tests for that kind of shit."

"Gee, I feel *soooo* much better now," I huff.

"Damn it, Ice. What did you expect? You left for two years. So, I got drunk and let some bitch suck my cock a few times. It didn't mean anything, the whole fucking time I had you in my mind. It was you I wanted."

"Surely you get why that doesn't fill me with happiness," I growl, still angry, but suddenly feeling exhausted.

"I get it, but I got to tell you that I'm really fucking pissed that your first instinct is to leave me. You did that once and almost destroyed both of us. When in the fuck are you going to grow up and face our relationship like an adult, Ellie?"

"I am facing our relationship like an adult," I mumble, but I'm lying and we both know it.

"Bullshit. Ever since you've came back, you've been hiding something. Don't even bother denying it. I see the look on your face when you think no one's looking. You look tortured. If you don't love me, if you don't want to be here, why in the fuck did you come back?"

"I came back because I love you. I want to be here, Liam."

"Then why won't you agree to have a baby with me? Why are you holding a piece of yourself from me? I can feel it, Ellie. I know you're not giving me everything. What the fuck is going on with you?"

"Well, it's a good thing I didn't give you all of me, isn't it Liam? Considering you've been giving it to Connie," I mumble.

"That's bullshit. You can be pissed about it, but you know Connie meant nothing to me, Ice. You also know that I have never wanted anyone but you. I saw you almost five years ago and all other women ceased to exist for me. You're it for me, Ellie. You've always been it. You're the one always running away. You're the one holding pieces of yourself away from me."

"I told you, Liam. I'm just not ready for a baby. There are things we need to—"

"Then stop putting it off, Ice. Tell me what I don't know. Let it out."

"I can't, Liam."

"You need to, Ellie. Tell me and we'll deal with it."

"Okay, I can, but I don't want to."

"Why, Ice?"

I swallow, my mouth suddenly feeling dry. I sit down on the bed, suddenly tired and feeling all alone. I look up at Liam and I know he can see the pain on my face. I don't try to hide it from him.

"I don't want to tell you, because once I do, you'll kick me out and you'll never take me back."

"Now you're talking crazy, Ellie," he dismisses me, but I don't blink as I look into his eyes.

"No, I'm not. I betrayed you, Liam and I know you well enough to know that you will never be able to forgive me."

I see the shock on his face. My nerves are churning in my stomach and I fight the urge to be sick. I hold my head down, suddenly wishing I could take it all back and keep my secret.

FURY

"What are you talking about, Ellie?" I ask, not sure I want to know the answer, but knowing that we can't move forward unless I do.

Of all of the things I thought Ellie would say, I never once thought she would tell me she betrayed me. She hasn't said what it is. It could be anything and the first thing that comes to mind is that she slept with someone else. Did Ellie cheat on me back then? If she did, can I get over it?

Fuck.

I watch as Ellie looks at me. I see her nerves. I see the way she's trembling. Whatever this is, it's big. I want to scream at her not to tell me. I don't know if I'll survive losing Ellie forever and suddenly that feels like what this is.

"Do you remember the week before you left to hunt down Vicki, Liam? Do you remember how sick I was? We thought maybe I had picked up the stomach virus from Ryan."

"I remember, Ellie," I tell her, because I do. It was one of the reasons that I didn't truly want to leave. It was my job and my responsibility, but I would have rather stayed home, making sure my girl was okay.

"I took a home pregnancy test, just on a whim. At the time, I remember thinking it was silly, but I did it and…it was positive."

I feel like the rug has been pulled out from under me.

"You were…" I have to stop, I clear out my throat try again, rubbing the side of my neck as I realize what she just said. "You were pregnant? Then, where's the baby, Ellie? Have you kept my child from me all of this time? Is that why you said you betrayed me?" I can't keep my voice steady, or the accusation from sounding harsh. I feel like I've been thrown in some fucking alternative universe, because this can't be coming from my wife's mouth.

"No," she cries. "I'd never keep your child from you, Liam, no matter what."

"Then, I guess you're going to have to explain this to me, Ice, because I'm fucking lost." I mutter, still unable to process what she's saying. There's a part of me that is upset there's not a baby and I can't begin to explain how fucked up that is.

"It turned out to be a false positive. I went to the doctor, because I wanted it confirmed before you left. I wanted to surprise you. I was crushed when I found out that I wasn't. I had already begun planning the nursery. I got my hopes up, even though I knew I shouldn't."

"Ice, I don't understand, what's going on here. Why didn't you tell me back then? What the fuck is this about?"

"I was going to tell you about the test, ask you if you could stay home at least one more day, because I was so crushed. I needed you to hold me and tell me it would be alright. But, you let it slip what you were doing, and what your job was."

"Fuck."

"You remember our fight," she murmurs. "I was so upset, Liam. My head wasn't in the right place. Then, I come to you, only to have you tell me you're off to end the life of a woman who was just trying to hold onto her son. I didn't like her, but I understood the need to hold onto her baby, because in that moment I wanted a child, I wanted the chance to be a mother, I wanted...*so much.*"

"Ellie, no." I almost moan the words, unable to process everything she's saying to me. She starts crumbling in front of me. I can see it, but I'm frozen where I am. I know she's getting ready to rip my heart out. I'm not stupid. There's a reason our intel was so good and then when I took off to Virginia to find Vicki, she just disappeared. She was like a ghost, which wasn't her style at all. I know what's coming next. *I know.* But, I need to hear it. "What did you do, Ellie?"

"Liam," she sobs.

"Tell me!" I yell. "What did you do!?!?!"

"She called the club to demand that Diesel bring her son to her. She was high, I could tell even through the phone. I told her she needed to get help. I warned her that if she didn't get clean, she didn't have a chance of ever getting her son."

"No, Ellie, don't tell me you...God, no, Ice." I'm begging her, even though I know it's useless.

"I told her you were coming, Liam. I told her she needed to get in a re-hab and disappear if she ever hoped to see her son again."

My eyes close. It feels as if my heart has been ripped out of my chest.

"You're the reason she went into hiding. You're the reason Diesel almost died..."

"Liam, if you just let me explain..." she says hopelessly, her body is heaving with the force of her sobs.

She reaches out to touch me and I recoil from her. I can't stop it. I walk out, leaving her alone and wondering if I ever really knew her at all.

ELLIE

$\mathcal{I}$ didn't realize a person could cry as hard as I did for that long a period of time. My eyes are red and they're burning. My head hurts, a migraine forming, but it's nothing like the pain in my heart, but my vision is blurry with it. I ignore it. I don't have a choice.

I knew once Liam found out the truth that he'd be angry. I thought maybe we could survive, but after seeing Liam's reaction and having him walk out on me, I know that we can't. I waited and waited for him, but it became clear he wasn't coming back. Now, it's the following day, the sun is just starting to come out and with no word from Liam... I know that I can't stay here. I take the letter I wrote him and fold it, putting it on our bed. Tears leak from my eyes again, but I wipe them away. I told Liam that I'd keep my cell with me. I begged him to forgive me and apologized again. It sucks, but I know that's all I can do. I hurt him. I betrayed him and I have to live with that. I knew better. As an old lady in the club, some things are sacred. It doesn't matter that I was upset and grieving, nor that I was sick of seeing Vicki throw away the child that I wanted so badly. Liam and I had been trying for over a year and it just never happened. I have endometriosis and we were told that getting pregnant would be a challenge. Getting that negative result after having my hopes up, nearly destroyed me. It's not an excuse, but my mind truly wasn't clear. If I had it to do over, I would. I wish like hell that I could.

But I can't.

There's nothing I can do but leave. Before I do that, there is one thing that I need to do. I leave my suitcase by the door as a wave of dizziness hits me. This headache is going to be my worst one yet. It's already amplified. It kind of feels like a sledgehammer is pounding against the back of my head.

I walk slowly to Diesel's door. There's a chance he and Rory are already moving around for the day, but I've noticed since I came back that Diesel spends time with Rory in their room early, and then goes to work with his brothers. I noticed it because I was happy for him. Before when I was here, I don't think he slept much at all. There were times when I doubted he ever used his bedroom. He'd fall asleep in his office most nights, or in Ryan's room on the floor.

I'm so upset that I actually pass up his door and knock on the wrong one at first. I'm not sure I would have realized it, if it hadn't been cracked and I looked inside, only to realize it was the laundry area.

I've got to get a grip. I just need to hold it together to talk to Diesel. After that, I can find a hotel and spend the day crying in bed—much like yesterday. When I finally make it to the right door. I knock, swallowing and trying to ignore the nauseous feeling in the pit of my stomach.

When Diesel answers the door, I can tell by his face that he's already spoken to Liam.

"Diesel," I murmur, curling my fingers into a fist and letting my nails cut into the palm of my hand.

"I thought you'd be around."

"You've talked to Liam," I respond, already knowing, but his tone is even. He's giving nothing away, but I can tell he's not happy.

"Did you think he wouldn't tell me?" Diesel asks, and I was wrong. He's not just unhappy.

He's mad.

"No, I knew he would, I was going to tell you myself. That's why I am here. I was hoping that maybe you would let me try to explain—"

"How you sold out the club and put my son in danger?"

"Noah," Rory says from inside. I can physically see Diesel put a cap on his anger, trying to reign it in.

Diesel backs up, opening the door wider, waving me inside.

Suddenly, I feel like I'm walking to my doom...

FURY

*Y*ou know you're a miserable fuck when alcohol doesn't dull the pain. I stare at the whiskey left in my glass, not really wanting another drink. I drank most of the night. It didn't help.

"You look like shit, Brother."

I pull my gaze away from my whiskey glass to look at Devil.

"Thanks," I mutter. I really didn't think it was possible to drink yourself sober, but I have. Either that or I've been staring at my next drink so long the effect of the others has worn off.

"How you doin', man?" he asks sitting beside me.

"Now's not a good time to ask me that, Devil."

"You didn't take my advice last night, did you?"

I frown, my grip on the glass tightens, but I still don't drink it. After I talked to Diesel, I sought Devil out. He's the man I'm closest to in the crew. I needed to talk to someone who could listen and help me sort through everything I was feeling. He tried, but it didn't help. His advice was to go back and talk to Ellie and try to sort shit out with her. I didn't do that, because I wasn't sure I could handle looking at her.

"I didn't," I confirm, still refusing to look at him.

i

"Stubborn as hell. A man has to be, but I'm thinking you got an extra dose," he mutters.

"She betrayed the club, Devil. Ellie was an old lady for over two years. She knew the rules. She knew what a fucking toxic woman Vicki was. She knew the hell that Diesel had gone through. How in the fuck am I supposed to overlook that she helped that bitch?"

"You aren't supposed to overlook it, but you might keep in mind that Ellie isn't a brother. She didn't swear an oath to this club, and she doesn't think like a man who has seen blood spilled does."

"Bullshit. She swore an oath to me, and I am the club," I growl.

"You and me. We see shit in black and white, Fury. There's good and bad and sometimes the bad has to be dealt with. Nothing in between."

"Devil, I really can't handle any heart to heart right now," I mumble.

"I think you get that when I met Torrent, she wasn't ready for me."

"Yeah."

"And even when I knew she loved me, instead of giving in to what we both felt, she tried to play devil's advocate and make sure no one was hurt."

"Devil—"

"Which kind of blew up in our faces, but still her heart was in a good place and she was letting her heart lead her decisions, which ultimately is what a good woman does, Fury. They lead with their heart, because that's where their goodness is. A good woman feeds your soul and she does that because of her heart."

"Fuck, man. Are you the one drinking here instead of me?"

"Just listen to me for a minute asshole. You and Ellie had been trying how long to have kids?"

"A while," I mumble, understating it. I knew that Ellie was beginning to give up hope. The doctor had been giving her fertility medicine and each month that went by, a little more of the light inside of her died.

"She got her hopes up and they were squashed. Then, she's faced with a fellow woman—"

"A conniving evil cunt," I spew.

"But, still a woman. A woman who had this beautiful son that Ellie would have died to have and she turns her pain loose, telling the woman to get help before it's too late."

"I know what she did, Devil. She warned the bitch. If she hadn't have done that, we could have gotten to her before she kidnapped Ryan and put him through hell," I growl.

"And, before I would have met Rory," Diesel says, coming up behind us. I turn to look at him. Telling him about Ellie's betrayal was one of the hardest things I've ever had to do. It's not exactly easy to look at him now. I think that's the reason Ellie's actions hurt the most. I owe Diesel everything. He brought me into this club and gave me a life. After getting back from overseas and seeing so much shit, suffering with PTSD, I felt like I was drowning. Being in the club gave me purpose again, and I began to heal from wounds that I wasn't even aware I had. I owe Diesel for everything I am now. To know that the woman I loved sold him out...

"Diesel—"

"I'm not saying it doesn't piss me off to know that the reason Vicki got away was more or less from my own club."

"There was no more or less. If Ellie hadn't told her to find a dry out and get her head together, we would have got her. The nightmare would have been over. Fuck man, Ellie's actions created so much fucking fallout. You almost died. How do you think I would have lived with that if you'd died?"

"How do you think I would have lived without Rory in my life, Fury?" he asks and I pull my gaze up to look at him.

"Because of Rory, Ryan is happy. He doesn't have nightmares. What he has is a life where he knows his mom would die for him and do it happily to protect him. My boy knows nothing but good now and that's because of Rory."

"Man—"

"And me? Fuck, Brother. I gave my club up. I walked away and went to Montana."

"And you did that because I wasn't able to shut Vicki down."

"I did that because I was tired, Fury. I was tired of being the president of this club. I was tired of living. I was turning cold and into someone that I didn't even recognize. I was someone who hurt a woman that I was growing to love. I was a fucking mess."

"That at least, I can understand," I tell him. "I'm definitely a mess," I mumble.

"If having Rory in my life means telling Vicki I was hunting her down and to go into hiding? I would have done it myself. I'd have told her exactly where we were looking. I'd have sold my soul if it meant I could have Rory when it was all over."

"That doesn't excuse what she did," I warn him.

"It doesn't, but in truth, what did she tell them, Fury? She didn't say anything to Vicki that I hadn't said to the bitch a hundred times over. I screamed at her that I was going to send men to hunt her down if she kept trying to get Ryan. I told her she needed to get her ass in re-hab. She just didn't listen. Chances are she didn't listen to Ellie either."

I look at my brothers and really try and consider what they've said.

"So, you want me to forgive her? You can deal with having her here in this club, knowing what she did?" I ask, shocked and confused as fuck. I also feel a little bit of hope beginning to grow.

"That depends," Diesel says. "Do you still love Ellie?"

"Of course I do. You can't just turn that shit off, Diesel. But—"

"The way I look at it, if I ban Ellie from the club, I'm going to lose my Sergeant of arms and I'm not prepared to deal with that shit."

"I...You..."

"You can tell me you wouldn't follow her to Phoenix or wherever it is she's packed to head out to, Fury, but we both know you'd be lying. You grieved for her for almost two years. I didn't notice it as much because of my shit, but I sure as fuck saw the difference in you when she came back. You were already planning on going to her then. I'm just stepping up before that happens again."

"You're serious?" I ask, feeling like a giant weight has been lifted off my shoulders. Ellie and I still have a lot to work through, but at least now it doesn't feel hopeless.

"I'm telling you the same thing I told Ellie when she came to my room to talk to me and Rory in person. Besides, my wife pointed out that I'd never made it mandatory that we don't talk things over with our old ladies. Our club is more relaxed than others—a fact she knows thanks to talking to Torrent," he says, giving Devil a pointed look.

"That's my Angel," he laughs.

"She *lovingly* pointed out that I couldn't get pissy now because ultimately it was my fault that I hadn't talked to my men about the issue before. A woman who was struggling to become a mother shouldn't have been expected to deal with all of the information she had. That's on me."

"And me," I admit. I slipped up and told Ellie too much. That's a big part of the problem.

"So, we work on those issues in the future—which hopefully won't happen because we won't have to face them," Diesel says. "Now, it's up to you, but Ellie was in bad shape earlier. Rory was worried enough about her, she talked her into staying in our room longer, and sent me to find you. Then, of course Torrent showed up with Cannon. That means you two need to go see to your women, so I can have mine back."

"I'll go find her."

"Good call. I'm going to go hunt Crusher and Dani down to collect my offspring," he says with a wink, walking off.

v

"Hey, Diesel?"

"Yeah, man?"

"Thanks."

He nods, Devil thumps me on the back, and I take off to find Ellie. It's not going to be easy, but I can't let her leave. Diesel was right. If Ellie was banned from the club, I'd end up leaving. There's no way I could go back to living without her.

I walk to Diesel's room, and just as I'm about to open the door, Ellie opens it, crying. For a minute, I'm afraid that things have gone south again.

"Ellie, I've got my keys, Torrent will tell the boys—Oh, Fury!" Rory gasps, surprised to see me.

"What's going on?" I ask, then my attention turns to Ellie. Her face is white, she has tears in her eyes and she's holding the back of her head.

"It's jut... st... just. Just a migraine," Ellie says.

"It's getting worse and she admitted her vision is blurry. I was going to drive her to the emergency room."

"She has meds, she gets migraines often, although they've slowed down lately. I'm sure she'll be..."

I stop talking as Ellie drops to the floor. I dive down to try and catch her, managing to get at least the upper half of her body in my arms.

"Ellie? Ice, wake up." She's out cold, looking abnormally pale.

"I'll call an ambulance," Torrent says, taking out her phone.

"Fuck that. I'm taking her," I growl. Panic spreads through me. She's never passed out before in her life. If the pain was so bad that she was stuttering earlier, something has to be seriously wrong. I can't wait for an ambulance to take her to the hospital, I can get her there sooner.

I pick Ellie up in my arms, carrying her toward the front door —praying that she's okay, and terrified that she's not...

FURY

I thought I'd been afraid before in my life. I've faced death with a gun aimed at me, I've watched my fellow soldiers blown to fucking pieces in front of me. I almost lost Devil, a man that is my true brother and family, same with Diesel. I've seen shit that gave me nightmares for years. But, not once, in all that time, have I ever been as scared as I am right now.

I made it to the hospital in a scary amount of time. I've never driven so fast in my life—and that's saying something. The entire ride, Ellie was completely unresponsive. I didn't know it, but they were waiting for us when we got here, Rory had called ahead. I'm thankful for that, because they immediately took her back.

I've been sitting here ever since, waiting. It's been at least twenty minutes and I'm not sure I'm going to survive much longer. Crusher, Dani, Torrent, and Devil showed up a bit ago. They had to have driven pretty damn fast themselves. They asked if I knew anything, but I just shook my head no. I'm not sure I can form words right now. We're all just...*waiting.*

"Mr. Maverick?" I jump up, looking at the woman coming out of the small door of the waiting room. She's wearing a white coat and scrubs. There's a large bright red streak on her coat and although Ellie wasn't bleeding when she went in, I'm terrified it's hers.

"That's me," I manage to say, my voice hoarse. I feel my family gather around me, leaving me thankful for their support. "Can you please tell me what's wrong with my wife?"

"We need to go in and do emergency surgery. I want to explain everything to you, but I don't have much time," she says.

"Emergency surgery?" I mimic, feeling like my fucking legs have given out on me.

"Your wife is bleeding on her brain. It appears she had an aneurysm that ruptured."

"How? I don't understand. She's not had any injuries. I want a second opinion."

"Mr. Maverick, I know you're upset, but time is of the essence here. The fact that your wife is still holding on is a miracle in and of itself. A lot of patients don't survive getting to the hospital. We already have her in the operating room. I need your permission and you need to sign the papers so that our surgeon can begin."

I never informed the hospital of our divorce. I was afraid they wouldn't tell me what was going on with her if I did. If she survives this shit, the first thing she's going to do is marry me again.

If she survives.

"Fuck, okay. Do whatever you need to do. Can I see her?" I ask, wondering how I'm still standing when my world is crumbling around me.

"I know you're worried, Mr. Maverick, but we can't delay. You need to know that Dr. Maples is the top in his field. We're very lucky to have him here. Your wife is in good hands."

I know she's trying to be reassuring, but she's not.

I walk like a robot to sign the paperwork they give me. I stay in that same trance as I go back into the waiting room.

"Fury, buddy, I know you're scared. I've been where you are now. There's nothing I can do or say to make you feel better, but look at my Hellcat. She's still giving me hell today. It's going to be okay. We don't fall in love with weak women. They fight tooth and nail to keep the life they love," he says.

His words hurt me, although he probably doesn't realize it. Will Ellie fight? She was getting ready to leave. I walked away from her, and I stayed away the entire night. Will she even know that I'm here? She was so confused, and looked so bad right before she passed out, that I can't know for sure she even knew I was there. I don't reply to Crusher, I just hold my head down, feeling useless.

Eventually, I take out my phone and look up Ellie's condition. Reading it now, it all makes sense. The constant migraines that seemed to be based behind her eye is a leading symptom. The harder fact to read is that fifty percent of people who have an aneurysm don't survive. Fifteen percent don't even survive the ambulance ride here. Then, there are the after effects. A lot of patients can suffer permanent neurological damage. My hands are shaking as I read all of this shit. Fear so deep that I can't breathe settles inside of me. My legs are constantly moving, as my nerves get the better of me. Twenty-five percent of all patients who survive the initial rupture can die within six months from complications. All these facts are assaulting me like physical blows, but, it's the triggers that can cause an aneurysm to burst that destroy me.

Fucking destroy me.

Strong emotions such as being upset or angry can raise blood pressure and cause aneurysms to rupture.

Being upset. Strong emotions....

I throw my phone across the waiting room. It slams against the wall and then drops to the cement floor. It lies there in pieces as I stare at it, wishing I could go back and take Ellie to the hospital when I first began to worry about the amount of migraines she had.

* * *

IT FEELS like years before the doctor finally comes out. When he does, my heart flips inside of my chest.

"Liam Maverick?"

"That's me," I respond, trying to gage what he's going to tell me by the look on his face, but I can't tell.

"Let's step into the consultation room," he says, but I shake my head no.

"This is our family. It's okay to talk in front of them."

"We've repaired the vessel in her brain. She's going to remain in ICU. I want to monitor her closely."

"Will she... Was there... Will she..."

Fuck, I can't even get the words out.

"Will she make a full recovery?" Devil asks, coming up beside me.

"It's too soon to say. The next couple of weeks are crucial. If all goes well, she'll need to have the metal plates removed in two weeks. In the meantime, we will need to monitor her to see if there are any neurological complications. I'm afraid I don't have a timeline for you, Mr. Maverick. We have to go at your wife's pace. I can tell you that she's strong and came through the surgery extremely well. She's definitely a fighter."

"Yeah," I murmur. "That's my Ellie."

"They'll come and get you when she's out of recovery and in critical care. You won't be able to spend much time with her. It's crucial right now she remain calm and have quiet. But I'll give you a few minutes with her."

"Thank you, Doctor."

He walks away and I'm left there with my brothers, Dani and Torrent, but I feel completely alone.

Please God, let her be okay...

ELLIE

 our Weeks Later

"You don't have to do this, Liam. I'll be fine in a hotel or..."

"Ice, stop it. This is your home," Liam says. Frustration and helplessness fill me.

"I don't want you feeling like you have to let me stay here. You aren't responsible for me, Liam. I don't want to be an obligation."

"Ellie, I love you. I know we have shit to work through, but we *will* work through it."

"Liam, I know I hurt you. I don't want you to keep me here because you're trapped. I'll be fine. You heard Dr. Maples, I'm doing extraordinary, all things considering."

I look at Liam, and I'm pretty sure he looks as ragged as I do—although he doesn't have one side of his head shaved. I haven't cut my hair or done anything with it, either. I think I'm afraid to, but I'm going to tackle it soon. What I hate the most is feeling like I'm this weight around Liam's neck. He's practically lived at the hospital, moving into my room as soon as I was put on the regular floor. There were some small complications, and that required a second surgery and me staying in the hospital longer, but I'm assured everything is fine now and truth be known, I am feeling better, I'm just really tired. It's just hard not to feel like you're walking around with a ticking timebomb in your head. I know I came close to dying and that's unnerved me more than anything.

"I've been telling you this for weeks and I don't think you've truly listened, Ellie."

"Liam—"

"So, I'm going to tell you again. We have problems, but we are going to work them out. We're going to learn to come to each other and talk, not run away, or in my case, ignore it until it's convenient. We're going to make this marriage work."

"We're not married," I point out, still afraid to believe him.

"That's a minor point, Ice. We're getting married this week."

"Oh no, we're not," I argue, my eyes going round with shock. I think he might be insane.

"We most certainly are," he says, coming over to the bed and going down on his knees, so that we are closer to eye level. "I almost lost you, Ellie. I've never been that scared in my life. I won't stay away from you. You're not moving out and that's the end of it." As he talks his finger brushes back and forth against my cheek and I close my eyes rapidly to stop the tears from falling. I seem to cry at the drop of a hat right now.

"Liam, I know you said we would put everything behind us and start fresh…"

"I was wrong," he says, causing me to frown in confusion.

"You were?" I ask.

"Yeah, honey. I don't want to put the past behind us. I don't want to forget one moment of our lives together. What I want is for us both to learn that we're stronger together and that's how we need to tackle everything."

"I…"

"Ellie," he says tenderly.

"I'm scared, Liam."

"I know, baby. But, you're going to beat this thing and I'm going to be right by your side."

"No, I mean, okay, I *am* scared about that, but I'm more worried about you feeling as if you're forced to be with me."

"Ellie, if anyone is being forced here, it's you. I practically had to kidnap you from the hospital to get you here."

"I fucked up, Liam."

"You did." I close my eyes as his forehead drops down to touch mine. "Ice, look at me." I slowly do as he asks. He pulls away far enough away so I can focus on him. "You fucked up, but I did, too. I should have stayed and talked things through with you all those years ago."

"You were under club orders, Liam."

"I fucking love my brothers, Ellie. I love this club, it's home, baby."

"I know..."

"But, Ellie, you're my world. I didn't show that to you back then. I even made it worse by letting you leave and not coming after you. I fucked up."

"I love you," I whisper, unsure of what else to say.

"And I love you. This is it, Ellie. Most people don't get a second chance. To my way of thinking, this is probably our third or fourth chance. We need to grab it with both hands and not let go."

"Together," I murmur.

"Definitely together, Ellie."

"You're not signing on to anything great, Liam. I look like something out of a Stephen King novel and you heard what the doctor said about—"

I stop when he puts his fingers against my lips.

"We fight like hell, together, Ice. You'll beat this because we have our whole lives in front of us. I want children with you. I want to grow old with you."

"I might not ever be able to have children, Liam, and with all of this…"

"Look at Dani and Crusher, Ellie. Do you think they look at that brood they have as anything less than theirs?"

"No," I admit.

"Let's take all of this one step at a time. Okay, baby?"

"One step at a time," I repeat.

"Hand in hand," he adds, his fingers brushing across my knuckles.

"Hand in hand. I'll never let you down again, Liam."

"We might let each other down, Ice. That's part of being human, but we'll work it out. Won't we?"

"We're still not getting married," I warn him.

"We are. The preacher is coming out to the club in two days. You are most definitely marrying me."

"Liam, I can't. I refuse to marry you looking like this."

"You're gorgeous," he argues, causing me to roll my eyes—even if it's painful.

"Will you be serious?" I huff.

"I am. I'm marrying you in two days, Ice. If you want a big wedding after your hair grows out, then we will do that. I'll do anything you want, but whatever happens, you are marrying me in two days."

"You're so damn bossy, Liam."

"Shut up and kiss me, Ice."

I finally just give up arguing. I guess I'm getting married looking like the bride of Frankenstein. I want to look beautiful for Liam, but we're together and he loves me. That is more than enough. So, I kiss him and send up a prayer of thanks. Somehow through everything we've faced, all of the wrong turns we've made, we ended up here…*together.*

EPILOGUE ONE

FURY

wo Months Later

"You about ready for bed, Ellie?"

She turns to smile at me, leaning against me.

"God, how I wish you were asking me that question to give me sex," she mutters, making me laugh.

"Soon, Ice."

"Easy for you to say," she huffs.

"Don't you believe it, Ellie. I'm aching for you."

"We could cheat and do it early. I won't tell my doctor if you don't," she suggests, but I shake my head no.

"Absolutely not. No sex until your doctor gives you the all clear."

"You better be resting up, Liam. Once I get healed up I'm going to wear you out."

"Now you're just teasing me."

"No, I'm warning you. I'm going to use your cock so much that it will be a miracle I don't break it."

"I always knew you were the perfect woman," I grin, leaning down to kiss her. Our kiss is long, slow, and full of frustration. We both definitely want more.

"A kiss like that should be followed by sex, Liam," she mumbles when we break apart.

"Would you settle for me carrying you to bed, snuggling in our pajamas and watching those horrible Christmas movies you like?"

"In a little bit? For now, I just want to stay here with our family," she replies and I smile at her. I look over at my brothers and their wives. It's a family dinner tonight and we've all moved out around the bar, soft music playing over the speaker.

They've all been so good to Ellie since she came back. I know she was scared, but things have just clicked into place. Diesel and Rory have been her biggest supporters, making sure she has everything she needs to be comfortable. I would have left all of them to keep Ellie in my life. When she first told me her secret, I thought I would be forced to do that. I'm glad that it didn't have to come to that. Because right now, I have everything a man could want and more.

EPILOGUE TWO

DEVIL

"*W*hat are you thinking, Logan?"

I look up at my wife. I was so lost in my thoughts that I didn't hear her come into the room. I reach out my hand to her and she takes it. I pull her down into my lap, leaning into her to give her a kiss.

"I was thinking that I'm probably the luckiest motherfucker on the face of the earth," I tell her when we break apart.

"I think that's my line," she whispers, her hand sliding against the side of my face. "I've put you through so much."

"You've given me the world, Angel. I'd go through it all again, just to be sitting here like this with you right now, surrounded by my family."

She curls into me deeper, her head going down to press against the side of my neck as she looks out at my brothers and their old ladies. Diesel and Rory are standing by the bar, laughing with Dani and Crusher. Down from them Fury and Ellie are talking to each other, their concentration on each other so complete that it's a toss-up on if they realize there are other people in the same room. Rebel and his new girlfriend are out on the dance floor, same with Scorpion and the woman he's been dating for the last month.

It's easy to tell that everyone here is happy and satisfied. I'm glad, I want that for my family, but there's no way in hell they are as happy as I am right now.

Torrent and I have come through hell, and through it all we've held onto one another. I wasn't lying to her, even though sometimes I wonder if she thinks so.

I'd go through every damn thing again, even Wolf's torture. I'd endure it all to be the bastard that gets to hold onto her like this, and be the man in her bed.

Life is sweet and fuck if it just doesn't keep getting sweeter.

"I love you, Logan."

"I love you, too, Angel. I always will."

We kiss then, and I realize that my brother Fury and I are just alike, because I love my wife so much that other people in the room cease to exist for me, too.

EPILOGUE THREE

DIESEL

$\mathcal{L}$ater That Night

"Noah, you've been quiet all night. Are you okay?"

I look over at Rory and give her a smile to reassure her.

"I'm good baby. I swear. I just have Ryan on my mind."

Rory walks over to the bed and slides under the covers. She's wearing one of my old t-shirts. I'd rather have her naked, but she doesn't like to sleep that way because of Ryan. He has a habit of coming into our room late at night. He doesn't do it as much now as he used to, but the possibility is always out there.

I tunnel my hand under the t-shirt and spread my hand against the warm flesh of her stomach.

"Ryan will be fine, you know," she says gently, those beautiful eyes of hers watching me closely.

"I know, it's just hard to let him go," I tell her. Ryan has a class trip tomorrow to the zoo in Ohio and a theme park. He and the other kids will be staying overnight in a hotel, and the thought of him being that far away from me makes me feel like I can't breathe.

"I thought that would be your reaction. So, me, being the perfect wife that I am—"

"You are the perfect wife," I tell her, leaning down to press a quick kiss against her lips.

"You do your best to never forget that, got it?" she says with a laugh.

"Trust me, I won't, Gorgeous."

"Good. Now, do you want to know what I've done that makes me the perfect wife?"

"I'm afraid that list is too long to go over, Baby."

"Keep that up, Noah and you're going to get lucky tonight."

"My dick is always up and ready when you're around," I joke and then laugh when she rolls her eyes at me.

"That was so bad. Don't make lame jokes like that when we're in Ohio tomorrow. They may kick us out."

"Ohio? But—"

"Dani is babysitting, Crusher will watch over the club while you and I go to Ohio as chaperones for Ryan's field trip."

"Chaperones? You're shitting me?"

"If you think I'm going to let our little boy go all the way to Ohio without us, you're crazy, Noah."

Our little boy.

As many times as she says that, I'm not sure I'll ever get used to it.

"I love you, Rory."

"I know and I love you, more. I'll always love you more."

As smart as my woman is, she's wrong about this. I don't argue with her, though. Instead I set about proving it to her with my body. In the end, I'm not sure I succeed, because she gives her body to me just as fiercely.

EPILOGUE FOUR

FURY

 *wo Years Later*

CHARLENE EVA LEE Maverick is perfection. There's no other way to say it.

I look over at the bed. Ellie is lying on her side and our little angel is snuggled up against her. Evie's features are so much like her mother, from her soft blonde hair, to the shape of her sweet face and her sweet blue eyes. She's smart, funny, inquisitive and happy. Hell, she's all of that and more and I'm definitely a proud father.

This past year has flown by and it's been all good. Ellie's recovery has been hard, but she has come through everything and remarkably has no real lasting aftereffects. We've worked on getting us where we need to be as a couple. It hasn't been easy either, but it was more than worth it. We're solid now, Ellie and I. Old ghosts have been put to rest.

We're raising Evie in a house right next to the club, and Ellie has completely embraced being part of the Savage Brothers. In fact, her, Dani, Torrent, and Rory are so tight that sometimes I think they're closer than I am with my brothers. We truly are a family and that brings me more joy than I could ever explain.

So long ago, I took one look at Ellie and knew that she was it for me. I wanted her forever and I knew beyond a shadow of a doubt that would never change. It hasn't. If anything, I'm even more certain. I never want to be without her. I live for her and Evie.

I lay down on the bed, as gently as I can, just needing to be close to my girls. My daughter remains sleeping, but Ellie opens her eyes at once. Her full lips spread into a smile as she looks at me.

"Liam," she whispers. That's all she says, but there's so much happiness and satisfaction wrapped up in the sound of my name that my heart squeezes in my chest.

"Missed you, Ice."

"I missed you, too. I'm glad you made it back."

"I couldn't handle not having you in my arms one more night," I respond, telling her the absolute truth. I've been in Chicago helping Gunner set up the new chapter of the Savage Brothers there. Rayne has been here visiting with Torrent quite often, but she loves living in Chicago. Gunner liked the idea of starting a new chapter. With some help from Diesel and Dragon, it's become a good place. The bonus is that Gunner is happier than I've ever seen him. Rayne is four months pregnant and I heard Torrent telling Devil that he needed to knock her up so their children would be the same age. Knowing Devil, he got to work on that right away.

"I'm glad," Ellie says, covering her mouth as she yawns. "I don't like sleeping in an empty bed."

"Ice, the bed doesn't look so empty right now," I tell her, grinning.

"Only for naps. She still sleeps in her crib. If she slept with us, I'm pretty sure I wouldn't get the fringe benefits my husband promised me if I remarried him. I can't jeopardize that," she jokes.

"Damn, I married a smart woman," I laugh.

"You're a lucky man," she replies, her grin deepening.

"Trust me, Ice. I know that."

Her face becomes almost serious as she stares at me. "Thank you for not giving up on me, Liam," she whispers, her voice tender.

"I think that's my line, Ice."

"I've been thinking," she says, her finger brushing in Evie's soft curls.

"Should I worry?" I ask, mostly kidding. I know that Ellie and I are solid. We've always been close, even when I found her in Phoenix after almost two years, we clicked back into place as if the time apart was nothing. But, since we worked out our past, we're close in a way that I didn't even know was possible. She tells me that we're soulmates. I never used to believe in that, but Ellie is definitely part of my soul, so I can't argue.

"I want another baby."

"Sweetheart, Evie is—"

"She needs a sister close to her age," she says, a crease forming on her forehead. I reach out and rub the frown, only wanting to see happiness on her face. I know she's thinking about Dawn. We don't hear from her anymore. Honestly, after Ellie confessed the ugly scene she had with her sister and mother, I'm glad. Ellie confessed she wonders if Dawn didn't have a hand in Glenna's death. After hearing that, I'd be lying if I didn't admit I like that Ellie doesn't have contact with her anymore. I know it hurts Ellie, but she's slowly coming to terms with it all.

"We'll discuss having a baby later," I tell her, not ready.

"Liam, you know Torrent will be pregnant soon. If you knock me up, we can go through pregnancy together."

"Later, Ice. We'll talk about it later," I tell her, knowing I'll give in, but still worried about her having a baby so soon.

iii

"Okay, but you just need to realize that if you drag your feet, Devil will outdo you."

"That's cold, Ice. You know I can't let that happen."

"I know." She grins and I shake my head.

"I love you, Ellie."

"I love you, too, Liam, and I'd show you, but...." She motions down at the sleeping Evie between us. I put my finger against Evie's hand, stroking her tiny, perfect finger.

"I wouldn't have it any other way, Ice." Evie's little fingers wrap around my much larger one, grasping it in her sweet little hold. It feels like my heart swells in my chest. "I wouldn't have it any other way," I repeat, my voice thick with emotion because my heart is so full...

It's overflowing.

JORDAN'S EARLY ACCESS

Did you know there are three ways to see all things Jordan Marie, before anyone else?

First and foremost is my reading group. Member will see sneak peeks, early cover reveals, future plans and coming books from beloved series or brand new ones!

If you are on Facebook, it's easy and completely free!

Jordan's Facebook Group

If you live in the U.S. you can **text JORDAN to 797979** and receive a text the day my newest book goes live or if I have a sale.

(Standard Text Messaging Rates may apply)

And finally, you can subscribe to my newsletter!

Click to Subscribe

SOCIAL MEDIA LINKS

Keep up with Jordan and be the first to know about any new releases by following her on any of the links below.

Newsletter Subscription
　Facebook Reading Group
　Facebook Page
　Twitter
　Webpage
　Bookbub
　Instagram
　Youtube

Text Alerts (US Subscribers Only—Standard Text Messaging Rates May Apply):

Text *JORDAN* to 797979 to be the first to know when Jordan has a sale or released a new book.

The Eternals

Eleven

Stone Lake Series

Letting You Go
When You Were Mine
Where We Began
Before We Fall

Filthy Florida Alphas

Unlawful Seizure
Unjustified Demands
Unwritten Rules
Unlikely Hero

Doing Bad Things

Going Down Hard
In Too Deep
Taking it Slow

Lucas Brothers

The Perfect Stroke
Raging Heart On
Happy Trail
Cocked & Loaded
Knocking Boots

Made in the USA
Coppell, TX
07 December 2019